PRICE OF HAPPINESS

Rich girl Tessa Ashton-Smythe was deeply hurt when her fiancé jilted her, admitting that her money had been the only attraction. So she changed her name to plain Tessa Smith and went off for a holiday as an 'ordinary girl'. And found that she still had just as many problems to contend with . . .

PRICE OF HAPPINESS

BY

YVONNE WHITTAL

MILLS & BOON LIMITED

15-16 BROOK'S MEWS
LONDON WIA IDR

First published 1977
Australian copyright 1982
Philippine copyright 1982
This edition 1982

© Yvonne Whittal 1977

ISBN 0 263 73984 8

Set in Linotype Plantin 11 on 12½ pt.
01-0882

Made and printed in Great Britain by Richard Clay (The Chaucer Press) Ltd, Bungay, Suffolk

CHAPTER ONE

THE hours spent at the piano, preparing for a recital, were always packed with tension for Theresa Ashton-Smythe, and it always reached its peak on the evening of the actual performance. When it was all over there was that incredible emptiness she had to contend with and the inevitable party to celebrate the success of the evening. This was what Tessa hated most—the champagne, the people milling about, and disembodied voices offering their congratulations, when what she wanted most was to crawl into bed in an effort to sleep off her exhaustion and, eventually, to find some way of eliminating the tension which had become a part of her daily existence.

'I want to *teach* music, not display myself on stage,' she had protested to her mother some days ago in a fit of pique.

'But you're so gifted,' her mother had argued, although she eventually agreed that Tessa had every right to do as she wished. 'It would be a pity, though,' she had been forced to admit.

Tessa was brought back to the present by someone topping up her glass of champagne, and she glanced up to see a young man smiling down at her. He had ventured backstage after the performance to offer his congratulations and, from that moment, he had been following her about quite brazenly since her arrival at the party.

'You're not enjoying yourself?' he asked, moving closer to her.

'Oh, yes,' she replied with a forced smile, escaping as gracefully as she could from the sudden intimacy in his eyes.

'Do let me introduce you,' one of the hostesses said as Tessa reached the other side of the room and found herself face to face with the one person she had hoped never to see again.

'We already know each other,' Jeremy Fletcher remarked, the familiar twist to his lips whenever he was nervous.

Strange that after more than a year she could still recall such little details about him, Tessa thought, her own face rigid with shock. Beside him stood a young woman. She was blonde and fragile-looking, and obviously out of her depth.

'May I introduce my wife, Meg,' Jeremy was saying.

Meg extended her hand nervously and Tessa, taking it, felt instant pity for her, and a certain warmth that made the rigid contours of her face relax into a smile.

'This is a surprise,' Tessa remarked with a calmness that surprised even herself as she glanced from one to the other. 'I never expected to meet you here.'

'I'm here as a representative for my company,' Jeremy explained, shifting his weight from one foot to the other. 'We arranged the booking of the hall and the seating accommodation for the recital.'

'Oh, I see.'

How civilised their conversation was, Tessa thought cynically. It was as if nothing at all had ever happened

6

between them. If Jeremy had been sincere all those months ago, *she* might have been standing there beside him as Mrs Jeremy Fletcher. It was a shattering thought she refused to dwell on. Meg's eyes were appealing as her hand searched for and found her husband's. It was obvious that Jeremy loved his wife very much and, strangely enough, Tessa did not envy her. There seemed to be nothing more to say. What was there to be said between them after all this time? Tessa excused herself as soon as she could and, to her horror, discovered that her legs were trembling.

Going home in the chauffeur-driven car some time later, she leaned back in her seat and closed her eyes. It was the end of May and in Johannesburg the winter months lay ahead with the promise of sub-zero temperatures at night and reasonably warm days. In the cushioned luxury and warmth of her father's car, she experienced none of the discomforts the late-night pedestrians were enduring.

This was what wealth did for you, she thought cynically. It gave you every conceivable comfort, yet at times, she longed to be a part of the average community who experienced happiness and a spontaneous gaiety despite the fact that they had to brace themselves against the winter cold.

The lights were on in the white-gabled and imposing Ashton-Smythe residence. Her parents had attended the recital, but had not remained for the party afterwards. They would be waiting up for her, she knew, yet this was one night she wished they had rather decided to neglect this usually pleasant interlude. Memories of the past were pressing to the fore, and she

7

had to be alone. Alone with her thoughts, however much they might hurt.

Philip Ashton-Smythe personally opened the heavy oak door to admit his daughter, and he led the way through the spacious hall with its crystal chandeliers and thickly carpeted floor. The central heating was on in the living-room with its panelled walls and cleverly concealed lighting, and Tessa shed her coat as she entered.

Her mother lounged in a chair, her still slender frame draped in a silk robe, her face glowing with pride. 'We're very proud of you, Theresa,' she said as she accepted her daughter's customary peck on the cheek, and Tessa smiled at her mother's insistence in using her correct name. She was the only one who had not succumbed through the years to using the abbreviated form of Tessa.

'You played exceptionally well this evening,' Philip remarked, handing them each a light sherry.

Praise from her father was indeed something. Although he played no musical instrument, he had an excellent ear and a fanatical appreciation for good music, and the rendition thereof.

'Thank you, Father,' she replied calmly, flashing him a little smile over the rim of her glass. She sipped at the crimson liquid and then something beyond her control made her say, 'Jeremy Fletcher and his wife were at the party.'

'Oh?' It came in unison from her parents, and she could sense the questions clamouring behind the forced casualness of their expressions.

'His wife's name is Meg,' she said in a stilted voice.

8

'She looks nice.' Concern mingled with casualness and Tessa, noticing this, abandoned her attempt at appearing uncaring. She drained her glass and placed it carefully on the marble-topped table beside her chair. 'If you don't mind, I think I'm going to bed.'

They did not attempt to stop her as she snatched up her coat and fled upstairs to her room where she stood for some minutes staring at herself in the full-length mirror. The white, fashionably designed dress clung softly to her slender, shapely figure, and against the tanned smoothness of her throat hung a diamond pendant set in gold. It sparkled as the light played across it and Tessa's lips tightened as she undid the catch and dropped it into the palm of her hand. Her hair was dark, almost black, and whereas she usually wore it hanging loose about her shoulders, it was now combed back and piled on top of her head, accentuating the slenderness of her neck with her head held proudly above it. Dark eyebrows were arched above crystal clear blue eyes that were fringed with equally dark eyelashes. Her nose was small and straight above perfectly chiselled lips that tilted at the corners, suggesting a hint of a smile.

While her mouth gave the impression of gentle submission, her small, square chin, with the slight dimple in the centre, suggested stubborn determination, and it was this determination which had been her crutch during the agonising time after ...

An angry exclamation passed her lips as she tugged at the pins in her hair, allowing it to cascade down to her shoulders. She changed swiftly, creamed off her make-up and slipped into bed, snapping off the bed-

9

side lamp to lie staring into the darkness. Memories forced their way back into the present, to the most disastrous day of her life, twenty months ago. Was it only twenty months? she wondered to herself. So much had happened since then. Her life had been so full; every minute taken up with her studies. There had been no time to brood, or lick the wounds inflicted. She had been grateful for this at the time, but meeting Jeremy so unexpectedly had brought past events cascading back into the present, and as vividly as if they had happened yesterday.

Jeremy Fletcher had asked her to marry him, and from that moment she had been walking on air. He had been her first love and, as she had thought at the time, her only love, and everything was going to be simply wonderful. She had been so ecstatically happy that she was oblivious of the slight withdrawal in his attitude towards her, and merely ascribed his manner to his reserved nature. As their wedding day approached, Jeremy became increasingly preoccupied, but then she had been rather edgy as well, and so, once again, she had thought nothing more about it.

Then, two days before the wedding, his letter arrived, and Tessa could still recall every word as if it had been engraved on her memory with a red-hot branding iron.

'Dear Theresa,' he had written, 'I am finding it extremely difficult writing this letter, but I realise there is no way I can possibly soften the blow, therefore I shall not waste time with platitudes.

Theresa, I was going to marry you for the money and position such a union would have afforded me, but I find now that I cannot go through with it. I have met someone whom I love very deeply. She is an ordinary girl from an ordinary family, and I realise now how despicable I was to have contemplated marrying someone as nice as yourself for your money alone. Money, after all, cannot buy happiness.

By the time you receive this letter I shall probably be married already, and I hope that you will find it in your heart to forgive me for the inconvenience and unhappiness I have caused you. Sincerely, Jeremy Fletcher.'

She could still recall the stunned silence which had settled on the living-room when she finally confronted her parents with the news that the wedding was off. They had stared at her as if she had taken leave of her senses.

Tessa rolled over on to her side, marvelling at the fact that she could recall everything with such clarity. Philip had removed his cigar from his mouth, dabbing at the corner of his lips with a clean white handkerchief. The ruby ring on his little finger had sparkled richly in the light of the table lamp as he placed his unfinished cigar in the ashtray with a jerky movement, and Tessa could remember drawing a similarity between that red flash of colour and the rawness of her emotions.

Sheila Ashton-Smythe had been the first to recover, her delicate eyebrows raised as she faced Tessa, who sat rigidly on the edge of her chair, her fingers playing nervously with the letter in her hands.

'This must be some sort of joke?'

'If it is, then it's a rather sick joke,' Tessa had said

harshly, choking back the tears. Her hand had trembled as she produced the letter. 'Read it for yourself.'

Philip had leaned closer to his wife as she unfolded the sheet of paper and their faces had paled visibly as they assimilated the contents together, while Tessa sat wringing her hands in anguish.

'How dare he! How dare he!' Philip had exploded, his face purple with rage as he paced the floor. 'I'll sue him. I'll break him financially!'

'No!'

A startled silence had followed Tessa's expletive. Her nerves had twisted themselves into a tight knot at the pit of her stomach as she faced her parents, her face chalk-white in the dimly lit room.

'But, darling,' Sheila had protested with concern as she returned the letter to Tessa, 'Jeremy must have known for simply ages that he had no intention of marrying you. Why did he wait until two days before your wedding to tell you? Why did he let us continue with the arrangements without saying a word? How could he be so inconsiderate?'

Without realising it, Tessa had sat tearing the letter to shreds between her agitated fingers. 'Knowing Jeremy as I do, I think he was driven by desperation to write this letter. He would never have had the nerve to tell me this to my face.'

'He's a coward,' Philip had observed angrily, 'and you're well rid of him!'

Tessa had flinched, but remained silent. No matter what Jeremy had been, she had loved him. Not even the knowledge of his insincerity, at that time, could have erased that fact. His letter had truly come as a complete surprise, and a tremendous shock.

'What are we going to do with all the wedding gifts that have arrived?' Sheila had wanted to know, her words cutting across Tessa's thoughts.

'Return them!' Philip's face had been a mask of suppressed fury. 'To think I could have been such a fool, as not to see through him!' His hands were clenched at his sides. 'If I could lay my hands on him at this moment I'd teach him a lesson he'd never forget!'

Tessa had flinched once more and Sheila, noticing this, had placed a silencing hand on her husband's arm before seating herself on the arm of Tessa's chair to place a comforting arm about her daughter's shoulders.

'Go to bed, darling,' she had suggested gently. 'It won't do any good trying to thrash this out at the moment. We'll talk again in the morning.'

Tessa had given her a thankful smile, then, as she rose to her feet, the remains of the letter cascaded to her feet.

'I'm sorry,' she had said hastily, stooping to retrieve them and at the same time making an effort to hide her tears. Her father's polished shoes had come into view and his hands gently lifted her to stand before him.

'Tessa, I wouldn't have wanted this to happen to you for anything in the world.'

Tessa could recall her inability to restrain the tears as they ran freely down her cheeks, and she had wept down the front of his expensive white shirt.

She had lain awake that night as she was doing at that moment; the only difference was that now her thoughts were no longer painful. Her mother had brought her a glass of milk on a tray that evening, and concern had deepened the fine lines about her mouth. At the sight of them Tessa had felt a pang of regret that her own heartache should have affected her parents so strongly. They had always protected and cosseted her; her problems had been theirs, and together they had always found a solution. But *that* problem had been hers alone.

'I've brought you a glass of milk and a tablet that will make you sleep,' Sheila had said gently, placing the tray on the bedside table and sitting down on the side of the bed while Tessa swallowed the tablet and drank the warm milk.

'Mother, I'm sorry I've caused you so much anxiety. If I hadn't been so blinded by my own love, I might have noticed that Jeremy was not sincere, but...'

'Don't think about it any more,' Sheila had interrupted, straightening the covers with her fingers and dropping a feather-light kiss on Tessa's brow. 'We'll talk in the morning. Now you must try to sleep.' At the door she had hesitated. 'Theresa, it's not the end of the world, my dear.'

Tessa sighed and forced her thoughts back to the present. She knew now that she had never loved Jeremy. It had been a romantic dream that was rudely shattered, and nothing more than her pride had been battered. However, the knowledge that he had contemplated marrying her for her money was something she still found unpalatable. It had shattered her faith in people, and had filled her with an uncommon bitterness and a growing doubt as to the sincerity of her friends.

An ordinary girl! Jeremy had married an ordinary girl from an ordinary home! The only thing that had attracted him to Theresa Ashton-Smythe had been the fact that she was the daughter of wealthy Philip Ashton-Smythe. This was the earth-shattering fact that Tessa had had to face, and which she still had to live with.

Surprisingly, Tessa slept well that night. Seeing Jeremy again had not been such an ordeal after all. It had merely brought back memories which no longer had the power to hurt her, except to awaken once again the desire to be accepted—and loved—for herself.

When Tessa later joined her mother for breakfast she found the newspaper beside her plate. Ignoring it, she poured herself a glass of fruit juice and buttered a slice of toast.

'The critics are very complimentary about your performance last night,' Sheila remarked enthusiastically.

'Are they?'

'Well, aren't you going to read what they have to say?'

'Later, perhaps.'

She could recall another occasion when her mother had not been so anxious for her to see the paper. Splashed across the front page in big, bold letters had been the words, 'Society Wedding Off'. There had been a photograph of herself and Jeremy, taken only a week prior to their supposed wedding, as they arrived at the theatre, and the accompanying item had begun : 'The wedding of the year between Theresa Ashton-Smythe and Jeremy Fletcher is off. The reason for the break-up of this much publicised romance is not yet known, but it is understood that Mr Jeremy Fletcher was seen to leave the city two days ago.'

The article had been spread over two columns as the reporter excelled himself in his report of their 'romance', as he had called it.

'Did it upset you very much to see Jeremy again?' her mother interrupted her thoughts.

'No.' Tessa frowned. 'It was a shock, that's all.'

'And it's brought back unhappy memories,' her mother guessed astutely.

'Mother, I realised quite some time ago that I never really loved Jeremy. I was in love with love, as they say, and I had a lucky escape from a disastrous marriage.'

'You seemed so upset last night.'

Tessa smiled reassuringly. 'It was merely shock at coming face to face with the one who had dealt my pride a shattering blow.'

'I'm glad.' Her mother wrinkled her nose. 'Glad, that is, that meeting him hasn't uncovered old wounds.'

Tessa laughed at her mother's discomfort and the subject was not discussed again. Her father joined them for breakfast moments later and read the reviews to Tessa while he had his usual eggs and bacon.

'What happens next?' he wanted to know as he pushed his plate aside and helped himself to a cup of coffee.

'Definitely not another recital,' Tessa protested. 'I'm exhausted!'

'Why don't you go on a cruise, or something?' Sheila suggested vaguely.

'Oh, I don't know,' Tessa mumbled ineffectively. 'I don't feel like going anywhere.'

'A trip abroad would help you regain your vitality,' Philip suggested helpfully. 'Why don't you take a long boat trip to Europe, do some touring and then fly back when you feel you've had enough?'

'I spent the whole of last year in Europe,' Tessa reminded him, becoming suspicious.

'Well, go anywhere you like, then,' Philip persisted.

'Are you trying to get rid of me?'

There was a guilty silence followed by self-conscious laughter. Sheila extended a hand across the table towards her. 'We don't want to get rid of you, darling, but we do feel that you should get right away from Johannesburg for a while. Perhaps out into the country where you can unwind at leisure.'

Tessa had to admit to herself that the thought of getting away for a while was tempting. If only she could go somewhere where no one knew her; where she would be accepted as just an ordinary person ... a nonentity.

An ordinary girl!

'That's it!' she thought, her eyes alight with pleasure as a plan began to materialise in her mind.

She rose quickly to her feet and planted a swift kiss on her mother's cheek. 'You've given me a marvellous idea and I'm going to start making arrangements immediately.'

She rushed from the dining-room and took the stairs two at a time on her way to her bedroom, leaving her parents to stare after her in complete astonishment.

That same day Tessa went on a wild shopping spree.

She needed clothes, but nothing elaborate. If she was to become just an ordinary girl, then her clothing would have to match her new status, and she certainly could not use any of the fashionably designed dresses that cluttered up her wardrobe. She caught a glimpse of her mother's startled eyes as she entered the house later that day with several parcels stacked on top of one another, the scarf on her head hiding the result of her visit to the hairdresser. This was going to be fun, she decided excitedly as she hastened to the privacy of her room to unwrap her parcels.

There were half a dozen off-the-peg dresses, one inexpensive chiffon evening gown for special occasions, several pairs of slacks with matching sweaters, one silky blouse she could not resist, a warm jacket and two baggy jerseys. The only item of luxury she would take with her would be her Porsche and, of course, her cheque book, as a mere precaution. She had withdrawn a sum of money that morning which should keep her for a month or more, depending upon circumstances.

From the passage cupboard she selected the two oldest suitcases. Their battered condition would add the final touch to her new image. She packed methodically, the excitement churning inside her. She had not felt so carefree and happy for a long time. This would be an adventure, and she was going to enjoy it to the full.

The only item she did not buy was shoes. She had enough well-worn, comfortable shoes to take along with her, she thought as she hummed to herself while moving about the room, completely engrossed in her task.

The masquerade would begin that very evening, she

decided as she selected a woollen dress and slipped it over her head. It was nearly time for dinner and she might as well confront her parents in her new disguise while informing them of her intentions. She dabbed some powder on her nose and touched up her lipstick, then stood back and regarded her reflection in the mirror with some trepidation. Would it work? she wondered.

Her long hair had been cut short and was curling softly about her face. This alone, she was sure, was going to upset her parents. The members of the press had always called her stunningly beautiful, yet in this inexpensive, ill-fitting dress she looked a little dowdy and no different from any other young girl of her own age. At that moment she certainly was not beautiful. To complete her disguise, she removed her rings from her fingers and replaced her expensive wristwatch with a cheaper one.

Laughter gurgled in her throat as she stared at herself. With her hair cut short and hardly any make-up on, except for a face cream with a light touch of powder and lipstick, no one would guess that the girl before them was Theresa Ashton-Smythe. At least, this was what she hoped for.

The dinner gong sounded in the hall and Tessa hesitated a few minutes longer. She wanted both her parents to be present when she made her entrance, and their reaction would tell her whether her efforts were futile or not.

Philip and Sheila were seated at the table when she entered. Philip half rose in his seat, his glance questioning, while Sheila stared blankly at her daughter for a moment before recognition dawned.

'Good evening, all,' Tessa said dramatically, spreading out her arms and dropping a light curtsy. 'Meet the new me—Tessa Smith!'

Philip sagged back into his chair. 'Tessa! What have you done to your hair? And those clothes?'

'How do I look?' Tessa asked, twirling about the floor. 'Do I look any different?'

'Different?' Sheila gasped, perplexed. 'If you weren't my own daughter, and if I didn't know you so well, I would never have guessed.'

'What's this all in aid of?' Philip demanded, pouring himself another sherry with trembling hands.

Tessa sat down opposite them. 'Take a good look at me. Will I be easily recognised? Mother, what do you think?'

'Well ... not at first,' Sheila admitted laughingly. 'But of course, if one took a closer look ...' She glanced helplessly at her husband. 'Philip? What do you think?'

'I think that whoever cut her hair made a mess of it,' he scowled, taking a sip of his sherry. 'What's all this in aid of, Tessa?'

Tessa placed her elbows on the table and cupped her chin in her hands. 'I'm going on the holiday you and Mother suggested. I'm going to get as far away from Johannesburg as I possibly can. I'm going to tour the countryside and see as much as I possibly can, and I'm going as plain, ordinary Tessa Smith.' She wrinkled her nose at her father. 'Do you think I'll go unrecognised?'

'I can't see why not,' Philip said at length, helping himself to some dinner, 'but why the elaborate disguise?'

Tessa's eyes clouded momentarily as she unfolded her table napkin and placed it on her lap. 'Father, I don't want to take any chances, and I don't want to be treated like Dresden china. I want to mix with ordinary people and I want to be treated like an ordinary person. Hence the assumed name, or partially assumed, Tessa Smith.'

'Where will you be going?' Sheila asked with a worried frown. 'Will it be safe for you to travel about alone?'

'Mother, I'm twenty-two,' Tessa remarked with slight exasperation. 'I shall, however, be taking along a fire-arm, and as for where I shall be going . . .' she shrugged slightly, 'I shall go wherever my fancy takes me. I'll send you a postcard occasionally.'

'When do you intend leaving on this trip?' Philip asked casually.

'Tomorrow at daybreak.'

'What happens if you're recognised?'

'Then I'll move on to the next place,' Tessa replied adamantly. 'I don't think I shall be recognised, though,' she ended hopefully. 'After all, no one will expect to see me in the small places I intend visiting.'

'Well, I wish you luck, Tessa Smith,' Philip remarked drily. 'You're going to need it, my dear. It isn't easy trying to pretend that you're someone else, you know.'

Tessa nodded, swallowing at the constriction in her throat. 'I know.'

If Philip and Sheila Ashton-Smythe were anxious about their daughter, they gave no sign of this as they saw her off the following morning. Tessa sighed with relief as she emerged from the city's boundaries and was at last on the open country road. She put her foot down on the accelerator and smiled to herself as the powerful engine of the Porsche responded magnificently. The Porsche had been a birthday present from her father and she had never been more excited about any gift than she had been about this one, despite her mother's fears that she might have an accident.

Tessa was heading for Natal where the South African winter would be more bearable, not that the winter months in Johannesburg were all that bad, for the days were quite warm despite the freezing temperatures at night. During June and July most people sped towards the Natal coast where the winter seemed milder, and the scenery more lush. Tessa had no intention of visiting the usual holiday resorts, but decided instead to call on lesser known towns where there would be peace and tranquillity among the hills and the winding rivers.

Tessa stopped for lunch at a road-house and at the same time had the Porsche's tank filled. This was not a planned trip and she still had no idea where she was going. 'I've never known a more disorderly person,' Jeremy had once told her in what she had thought was a loving voice. She was not generally a disorderly person, yet she hated planning ahead to the last detail. Jeremy had been just the opposite. Everything always had to be planned for tomorrow, the day after, and every other conceivable day, and quite often he had had to face his disappointment when his plans went awry. Tessa preferred to take every day as it came. It was so much more exciting. Oh, bother Jeremy! Why did she have to think of him now?

She turned off the main road and on to a secondary

road later that afternoon, and her only reason for choosing that road was that it looked as though it would lead to something interesting.

She came to a small town later that afternoon which seemed rather deserted, and there was no difficulty in acquiring a room for the night at the small but spotless hotel. After parking her car for the night, she took her overnight bag up to her room and bathed and changed before going down to dinner. Her table companion was a young girl who taught at the local primary school and Tessa, who would have preferred to dine alone, spent a few tense moments in her company until she realised that the girl had no idea who she was.

'Are you on holiday?' Tessa's companion asked conversationally.

'Yes.'

Her reply had been rather abrupt, the tension increasing as she realised that she was about to be questioned intensively.

'I see you come from Johannesburg,' the girl continued, mercifully not upset by Tessa's distant attitude. 'Do you live with your parents, or do you have a flat?'

'I have a flat,' Tessa replied hastily. This in itself was not entirely a lie, for her rooms in her parents' mansion was tantamount to a flat. She had her own bedroom, bathroom and living-room in the east wing of the house although they always shared their meals together as a family, and this had been the arrangement since she had been in her teens.

'In Hillbrow?' the girl asked, her eyes wide and enquiring.

'No, not in Hillbrow,' Tessa had to laugh. 'It's obvious that you've been hearing stories about life in Johannesburg, and especially Hillbrow.'

The girl put down her knife and fork and leaned across the table. 'What's it really like in Hillbrow? Is life really as wild there as they say?'

Tessa looked across at her table companion and found it difficult to suppress the smile that hovered about her lips. 'I would say that Hillbrow is the most densely populated area in Johannesburg, and as for being wild——' Tess raised her eyebrows a fraction. 'Hillbrow is a very cosmopolitan area, but I wouldn't exactly say that life there was wild.'

'Do you go there often?'

'Not often, no,' and as if to signify that the conversation should be concluded, Tessa concentrated on her dinner. She was not in the mood for lengthy discussions, not yet, and this girl was obviously hungry for conversation with someone of her own age. She felt sorry for her, but she could not relax sufficiently to enjoy her company.

Tessa saw the young schoolteacher only briefly at breakfast the following morning and she was thankful that she had slept rather late before going down to the dining-room.

'Enjoy your holiday,' the girl said as she gathered up her books, 'and think of me slogging away in the classroom while you're lying on the beach.'

She had naturally assumed that Tessa would be going to the coast, and Tessa did not contradict her as they bid each other goodbye. At the towns along the coast there would be newspapers and reporters, and this Tessa wanted to avoid at all costs. She was not so certain that her disguise was all that good and she dreaded the thought of being discovered.

She drove at a leisurely pace that day. There was no hurry and there was no specific destination she had to reach at a certain time. It was rather late that afternoon when she found herself travelling along a winding road amid the sugar cane plantations. She would have to find a town soon or she might find herself driving about in the dark, which was something she wanted to avoid. She pulled off the road and consulted her map. To her horror she discovered that she had no idea where she was. She had merely driven along without even taking note of the signposts, if there had been any, with the result that she was now hopelessly lost.

'Thoroughly disorganised,' she admonished herself as she flung the map angrily on to the back seat. There was now only one thing to do, she decided, and that was to turn off to the nearest farm and ask directions. Goodness knows what the people would think of her, but unless she wanted to continue driving round in the middle of nowhere, she would just have to stop and make a few enquiries.

Five kilometres further down the road she noticed a farm track turning off to the right. The board attached to the gate had the name 'M. D. Craig' printed on it, and Tessa could only pray that M. D. Craig, whoever that might be, would not think her completely idiotic. The road had been cleared of sugar cane on either side, Tessa noticed as she bumped along in search of the house. Driving at such a slow speed the interior of the car became hot, and the perspiration broke out on her forehead. Her discomfort would have to be tolerated for a while longer until she had obtained the necessary directions to continue her journey.

The house was soon in sight and it was not at all the kind of house Tessa had expected. Contrary to the colonial-style houses she had encountered along the way, this house was low slung and modern, and built on a hill with the garden sloping down for an immeasurable distance. The lawns were green, and in amongst the rockeries the succulent plants flourished. The garden contained mostly shrubs, which meant that it needed very little attention except for mowing the lawns in summer and the trimming of the edges. It was nevertheless pleasing on the eye.

Tessa hesitated a moment before turning up the long drive towards the house. What kind of reception would she receive? she wondered. 'He who hesitates is lost,' she thought wryly, and she was well and truly lost. Worse still, the sun was sinking swiftly. She accelerated and moments later the Porsche was parked at the front entrance to the whitewashed house with the polished stone patio and the ivy creeper trailing along several of the carved pillars.

She was about to emerge from the car when she noticed someone coming towards her. He was one of the most striking men she had ever seen. Tall and broad-shouldered, he was dressed in tight-fitting denims and red shirt. His fair hair was bleached even whiter by the sun, and his skin was tanned to a deep golden-brown. He was obviously in a hurry, for he approached her car with a firm, purposeful tread and opened her door to help her out.

Tessa looked up into a pair of glittering green eyes

26

and promptly lost her voice as she allowed herself to be ushered towards the house without a word being spoken between them. This man, whoever he was, was obviously in a foul mood, and Tessa, curious at her own lack of speech and the disturbing sensations caused by the touch of his hand beneath her elbow, found herself being propelled mutely across the paved patio and through the double oak doors into the entrance hall with its atmosphere of cool sophistication.

At the door to his left he hesitated a moment and Tessa miraculously found her voice. 'I was wondering ...' she began hesitantly, only to be interrupted rather abruptly.

'My mother will gladly answer all your questions. I haven't the time, nor the inclination,' and with that he opened the door and once more propelled her forward.

CHAPTER TWO

IN THE comfortable armchair beside the window which overlooked the garden sat an elderly woman, her grey hair combed back and rolled into a bun at the back of her head. Her one leg was in plaster and stretched out before her, her foot resting on a small leather pouffe. Tessa stared down into a pair of startled eyes and felt her heart beating uncomfortably against her ribs. Her decision to stop and ask the way was developing into something rather frightening, and altogether puzzling.

'Miss Emmerson has arrived, Mother,' the man said beside her in his deep, well-modulated voice. 'I'll leave you to explain the details.'

'But this can't be possible!' the elderly woman gasped, her eyes taking in Tessa's appearance from her dark head to her comfortable leather shoes and then back to equally startled blue eyes. 'I've just been speaking to Miss Emmerson on the telephone. She told me that she wouldn't be able to take up this position as housekeeper-companion as her own mother has become seriously ill.'

'Then who the devil are you?' the man asked, swinging round on Tessa with such fury that she involuntarily backed a step.

'I—I'm Tessa Smith.'

She glanced at the woman in the chair and was on the verge of stating her business, when she saw a peculiar smile lurking in the eyes of the woman before her.

'You must be the replacement Miss Emmerson mentioned,' the woman said gently, and Tessa experienced the sensation of sinking into quicksand. What was happening? She had merely wanted to ask the way, and in a short space of time she had been mistaken for the housekeeper-companion, and before she could dispute this fact she was being mistaken for the replacement.

'You *are* the replacement, aren't you?'

Tessa stared helplessly down into green eyes similar to those of the man standing rigidly beside her, and it was as if a message of appeal was being flashed in her direction. Before she could prevent herself, she had replied in the affirmative.

'Good,' grunted the simmering volcano beside her. 'I'll leave the two of you together then to sort out the preliminaries.'

Without another word he strode from the room and left the two women alone. Tessa stood for a moment and stared about her. The furniture was modern and comfortable, the paintings on the walls obviously genuine, and once again there was that air of sophistication one would not expect to find in a farmhouse. Her swift glance did not miss the upright piano standing at the other end of the room, and she wondered curiously whether it was a mere ornament.

'I suppose you think we've all gone mad?' a gentle voice interrupted her thoughts, and Tessa once more glanced down at the woman before her. A smile curved her lips and lit her eyes to a glittering green, so like the eyes of the man who had unceremoniously ushered her into the house.

'I admit the thought had crossed my mind,' Tessa remarked, a smile quivering on her own lips. 'I'm afraid

I stand before you under false pretences. 'I'm not the lady sent as a substitute for the one you'd hired, and I merely wanted to ask the way. I'm on a touring holiday and I'm afraid I've lost my way.'

The woman nodded, clasping her hands together in her lap. 'I can tell you where you are. You're in the heart of the sugar cane country, about thirty kilometres from a town called Idwala, which is the Zulu name for a large rock. The town is built at the foot of a hill that has the formation of a large rock, hence the name.'

'Thank you very much,' Tessa sighed with relief as she prepared to take her leave. 'I'm sorry I had to trouble you, but now that I know where I am, I shall be on my way.'

'Just a minute. Aren't you forgetting something?'

Tessa turned slowly. 'I don't think so.'

The woman smiled lazily. 'You admitted, in front of my son Matthew, that you were the replacement for Miss Emmerson who, unfortunately, couldn't come.'

Tessa laughed briefly to cover her anxiety. 'That was merely a joke, I presume.'

'I was serious.'

The silence in the room was suddenly deafening. This was positively ridiculous, Tessa thought frantically. She had no intention of hiring herself out as a housekeeper-companion to *anyone*, not even to this woman with the gentle, probing eyes who was incapacitated by the enormous plaster on her leg.

'Mrs ... er ...' Tessa floundered.

'Craig. Ethel Craig, and it was my son, Matthew, who ushered you in here so ungraciously.'

Tessa ignored the last part and plunged into speech.

30

'Mrs Craig, I can't possibly stay here as housekeeper-companion.'

'Why not?'

The directness of the question startled Tessa and left her momentarily speechless. 'But ... but I'm not ...'

'Yes, I know,' Ethel Craig laughed. 'You're not qualified to do that type of work, but I like you and I think you may find we have much in common. I would rather have you than anyone else Matthew might decide on.'

'But you don't know me!' Tessa protested desperately. How on earth was she going to get herself out of this situation? she wondered. This woman appeared to be blocking every avenue of escape and, instead of becoming frantic, Tessa found herself liking Mrs Craig more with every second that passed.

'Perhaps I should explain,' Ethel Craig began calmly. 'I did a very foolish thing last week. I fell from the ladder in the pantry and broke my leg. After this happened, Matthew decided that I should employ someone to help me in the house, someone who could also take care of my personal needs and keep me company while I'm virtually chained to a chair. If my son seemed abrupt when you arrived, it's because he hates the idea of strangers in the house, but he considered it a necessary evil at present. When Miss Emmerson telephoned to say that she couldn't come, I shuddered to think who Matthew might replace her with.' She leaned forward confidentially. 'I didn't like very much of what I saw of her, you see. However, I had hardly replaced the receiver when *you* arrived, and Matthew, thinking that you were Miss Emmerson, brought you to me.' Her glance swept Tessa from head to foot. 'I like you,' she said candidly, 'and I think I could bear to have you around me all day long. Won't you stay? I shall pay you well.'

Ethel Craig mentioned a sum that made Tessa's eyes widen with surprise, knowing that any ordinary girl would not think twice at accepting the offer. An ordinary girl! Tessa flinched inwardly. Was that not exactly what she was trying to be—just an ordinary girl? She shook herself slightly as she hovered on the brink of accepting. She had planned a touring holiday, not a working one . . . and yet . . . why not? It might be fun, and it would at least be different, despite the disapproval in the glittering green eyes of Matthew Craig.

'Mrs Craig,' Tessa began slowly, choosing her words carefully, 'I'm afraid I have no experience at all for this job you're offering.'

'Can you cook?' The green eyes appraised her intently.

'Yes, but——'

'Then it's settled.' Ethel Craig rang the bell beside her chair and moments later the door opened to admit a Zulu servant girl in a green overall and starched white apron. 'Will you take Miss Smith's suitcases to the room we've prepared for her?'

Tessa, surprised by her own reluctance to contradict this woman, turned to follow the servant girl.

'Miss Smith!' Tessa turned sharply, expectantly. 'Not a word to anyone about our conversation. You arrived here as Miss Emmerson's replacement. Matthew especially must not know the truth.'

Tessa's heart knocked heavily against her ribs. Matthew Craig was obviously someone to be wary of, but perhaps their paths would seldom cross, she thought.

'I shall remember, Mrs Craig.'

'And come back here when you have settled in.'

Tessa smiled and nodded. Later, her suitcases unpacked, Tessa stared at herself in the mirror. 'Have you gone mad, Theresa Ashton-Smythe?' she asked herself sarcastically. 'Couldn't you have put your foot down and refused adamantly to become involved in this situation?'

She shook her head at herself and wondered what her parents would think of the situation she had become involved in. What if the Craigs discovered her identity? And what if Matthew Craig discovered that not only was she not the replacement for Miss Emmerson, whoever she was, but that she was actually someone else as well, and not Tessa Smith as she had told them?

A tremor went through her as she looked about her. There was nothing elaborate about the room she had been given. A rose-coloured carpet adorned the floor and the curtains and bedspread were of a matching colour. The wardrobe and chest of drawers were of a solid dark wood, and also the dressing table with its large mirrors. Against the one wall stood a single bed with a padded headboard, and beside it a small table with a reading lamp placed on it. The room, in fact, displayed a simplicity that was welcoming.

Tessa went across the passage to the bathroom the servant had pointed out to her and sponged her face and hands before returning to her room to change. The sun had set and yet the warmth of the day lingered on, so she selected a colourful cotton frock, powdered her nose and touched up her lipstick before returning to the living-room where Mrs Craig was awaiting her.

'Ah, here you are,' she smiled, pointing to the chair close to her own. 'Please sit down and let's talk.'

Tessa sat down gingerly on the edge of the chair, more than aware of what was to follow. Ethel Craig regarded her for several minutes in silence before a smile once more lit up her face. Tessa felt uneasy under her surveillance, but had withstood it remarkably well, she thought to herself.

'Miss Smith ... er ... what did you say your name was?'

'Tessa.'

'Yes ... Tessa.' She glanced at her questioningly. 'Where are you from?'

Tessa hesitated only a moment. 'Johannesburg. Why?'

Ethel Craig shrugged her shoulders lightly. 'I just wondered.'

Tessa bit her lip nervously. 'Mrs Craig, you're taking an awful chance employing me. How do you know I'm not an unsavoury person?'

Again there was that peculiar smile that lit her eyes. 'You have a cultured voice, Tessa Smith, that's pleasing on the ear, and it also tells me that you've had a good education. You also carry a great sadness in your heart that's reflected in your eyes.'

This woman was far more astute than Tessa would have guessed and it was not going to be easy pulling the wool over her eyes. This venture had suddenly become a challenge to Tessa, and despite her misgivings, she intended to go through with it.

'Won't you tell me what has caused your unhappiness?' Mrs Craig asked gently.

Tessa lowered her glance and gripped her hands together tightly. 'If you don't mind, I would rather not.'

Mrs Craig accepted this resignedly. 'Perhaps one day, when the hurt is not so prominent, you will tell me?'

'Perhaps,' Tessa agreed. 'For how long will you require my services?'

'For six weeks, I think, until I'm able to get about without assistance.'

For several minutes they discussed the job Tessa had accepted and then Mrs Craig told her something about herself.

'My husband died several years ago and ever since then Matthew has taken over the farm,' she informed Tessa. 'I have two sons. Matthew is thirty and the elder, then there's Barry who's six years younger. Both my sons are here on the farm, although Barry doesn't care much for the idea of remaining here. He would rather go to the city, but Matthew is determined that he should remain here. You may have guessed that what Matthew says is law,' Mrs Craig laughed lightly, 'but he's sensible like his father used to be, and he generally knows what's good for all of us.'

'Aren't there clashes between the two brothers?' Tessa queried. 'Barry is apparently of age and at liberty to make his own decisions, and yet he allows Matthew to rule his life?'

'There are clashes occasionally,' Mrs Craig admitted ruefully, 'but Barry is gentle-natured and not as forceful as his brother. Barry is also rather careless and scatterbrained, like myself, and Matthew feels that until Barry is able to start behaving sensibly, he should remain here on the farm where he can keep a watchful eye on him.'

'Are you unable to get about at all?'

'I have a wheelchair,' Mrs Craig pointed to the chair placed out of sight in the corner of the room. 'I get about quite comfortably in that, in fact I think you should help me into it so that I can show you the house.'

'Won't your son object?' Tessa asked hastily, fearing the wrath of Matthew Craig whom she had, as yet, met only briefly.

'Matthew won't object, and don't let him frighten you or bully you,' Ethel Craig advised humorously.

Tessa brought the wheelchair closer to Mrs Craig's chair and helped her from the one to the other. Fortunately the woman was slenderly built and Tessa had no difficulty in assisting her. She wheeled her from the living-room and down the passage, and in this peculiar fashion Ethel Craig took her on a tour of the house, until they eventually landed up in the kitchen. One glance at the old-fashioned coal stove made the blood in Tessa's veins turn to ice.

'Is—is that what you cook on?' she stammered, her eyes riveted to the object she had thought no longer existed.

'Yes. It's very simple, really,' Mrs Craig remarked calmly, and went on to explain the intricacies of cooking, in what Tessa thought was a primitive fashion.

'Am I expected to start cooking as from this evening?' Tessa asked with a breathless note in her voice.

'The sooner you acquaint yourself with your surroundings, the better,' Mrs Craig grinned humorously.

'Daisy,' she gestured towards the Zulu servant girl peeling potatoes at the table, 'will explain whatever you need to know.'

Tessa glanced down at her employer speculatively. 'Mrs Craig, I wonder if you realise what you've taken on?'

Laughter twinkled in her employer's eyes. 'Take me back to the living-room, young woman, and get to work!'

And get to work Tessa did. By the time the dinner was ready to be served, Daisy sighed an audible sigh of relief, which Tessa echoed thankfully. There was a black smudge across her forehead, her nose was shining, and her cheeks were flushed from bending over the hot stove. She felt a mess, and was certain she looked it too.

'Well, hello there!'

Tessa swung round sharply to see a young man standing in the outer door. He had dark brown hair, and laughing grey eyes that were regarding her with undisguised interest.

'Don't tell me you're the redoubtable Miss Emmerson we've all been dreading to meet?' he asked, sauntering towards her.

'I'm Miss Emmerson's replacement,' Tessa lied glibly, crossing her fingers behind her back.

'Then may I say welcome to our humble abode, Miss ... er ...'

'Smith,' Tessa replied calmly.

'Smith?' His eyes widened comically. 'And your other name?'

'Tessa.'

37

'Tessa.' He rolled her name around his tongue almost in the fashion of a wine taster. 'I like it. May I call you Tessa?'

'You may,' she replied, not quite certain how to react towards this newcomer.

The young man bowed melodramatically. 'Miss Tessa Smith. I'm Barry Craig, at your service, and may I say that I hope your stay will be a pleasant one for all concerned. I for one am delighted that Miss Emmerson couldn't come after all.'

A glimmer of a smile hovered about Tessa's lips. 'Do I take that as a compliment, or are you in the habit of flattering every woman you meet?'

He crossed his hands over his heart and feigned an injured expression. 'You do me an injustice, I assure you.'

'I wonder,' she murmured softly, excited at the thought that, for the first time, she was being treated like an ordinary girl.

'When do you have a free evening?'

'Mr Craig, I've only just arrived,' Tessa protested laughingly.

'Does that make a difference? And the name is Barry, by the way.'

Tessa stood for a moment at a loss for words. 'I'm in your mother's employ,' she began hesitantly, and the next instant the outer door flew open to admit Matthew Craig, and there was no mistaking the menacing look on his face.

Barry took one glance in his brother's direction and, with a muttered exclamation, he hastily left the kitchen. Tessa faced Matthew Craig with the curious feel-

ing that she had erred and she clasped her hands together behind her back in a childish fashion, and waited.
The straight nose, firm lips and square chin denoted
strength, while the green eyes sparked disapproval.
Tessa had to admit to herself that he was very attractive,
in a rugged sort of way, and his presence had the most
peculiar effect on her nerves, almost as if he were
touching her. At this point she made a strenuous effort
to shake off her disturbing thoughts.

'Miss ... er ... Smith,' Matthew Craig began, his
voice ominous, 'you have been employed as housekeeper-companion to my mother, and not for the purpose of entertaining my brother.'

'But, Mr Craig——'

'I would be grateful if you would remember your
position in this house in future,' he cut across her words
with an abruptness that stung, and without a further
glance in her direction, he strode from the kitchen, his
footsteps echoing down the passage.

'How dare he speak to me like that!' Tessa thought,
anger vibrating through her, and then she caught herself up sharply. A new helplessness seized her as she
remembered her new status. She was now merely an
employee, and that was something she would have to
remember, as Matthew Craig had informed her, but
not even this realisation could entirely evaporate her
anger. He was arrogant and rude, and she hated him!

Despite Mrs Craig's insistence that Tessa should
join them for dinner in the dining-room, Tessa remained adamant about eating in the kitchen. Matthew
Craig had instructed that she should remember her
place, and remember it she would! He had the power

to anger her, and in a moment of anger she might be tempted to reveal her true identity, and this was something she wanted to avoid at all costs. The less she saw of Matthew, the better, she decided firmly, yet this was going to be difficult when they had to live under the same roof.

After dinner that evening Tessa assisted Mrs Craig as she prepared for bed. It was a new and joyous task for Tessa, and for the first time in her life she felt that she was doing something useful. When Ethel Craig was settled comfortably against the pillows, Tessa turned to leave.

'Don't go yet,' her employer begged. 'Stay a while and talk to me.'

'I thought you might want to read.'

Mrs Craig gestured impatiently with her hands.

'I have all day to read if I wish. Stay and talk to me, child, or I shall go mad with boredom.'

Tessa sat down in the chair beside the bed and smiled sympathetically at the older woman. 'I'm afraid that as a companion I shall fail you miserably. I'm not a very wonderful conversationalist. I haven't had much practice, you see.'

Ethel Craig was shaking with silent laughter as Tessa glanced at her. 'You are, at least, honest and original, Tessa,' she laughed. 'There must be several questions you want to ask, so why not make that a starting point in our conversation this evening?'

Tessa clasped her hands nervously in her lap. 'Won't you think me rude?'

'My dear Tessa,' Ethel sighed exasperatedly, 'I'm giving you the opportunity to ask questions, am I not?'

Tessa nodded and relaxed slightly. 'How many years

40

have you lived here on this farm?' This was a silly question, but she could think of nothing else at that moment.

'For thirty-four years. Almost a lifetime, you would say,' she added as Tessa's eyes widened.

Tessa looked about her with interest. 'This isn't an old house,' she observed almost to herself.

'You're quite right, this isn't an old house,' Mrs Craig admitted. 'Four years ago the sugar cane caught fire and the wind blew a spark on to the thatched roof of the house, and ...' she gestured expressively with her hands, 'the house burnt down to the ground.'

'Do you often have fires in the cane fields?' Tessa asked with interest.

'Not often, but occasionally it does happen.'

Tessa could hear Matthew's raised voice somewhere in the house and instantly tensed. 'Does your son hate the idea very much of having someone like myself in the house?'

Ethel Craig laughed then. 'He abhors the idea but, as I said before, he considers it a necessary evil.' She stared intently at Tessa for a moment. 'Don't let his attitude trouble you. He'll get used to the idea eventually.'

'Who will get used to what idea eventually?' a voice demanded from the doorway, and Tessa leapt from her chair as if she had been shot.

Mathew Craig sauntered into the room, bringing with him an aura of masculinity that disturbed Tessa and sharpened her senses. He had exchanged his denims and red shirt for a pair of cream-coloured flannels and a dark green shirt that matched his eyes ... eyes that seemed to take in every detail of her appearance as they

41

flickered momentarily in her direction.

'Matthew, how nice of you to come and chat,' Ethel smiled, patting the side of her bed. 'Sit down for a moment.'

'You haven't answered my question,' he said, seating himself beside her and glancing at Tessa as she hovered on the verge of flight.

'I was merely stating that I would eventually get used to the idea of being a semi-invalid for a time,' Mrs Craig covered up smartly, her glance never wavering.

'If you'll excuse me——' Tessa muttered, making for the door.

'Miss Smith!'

Tessa stopped dead in her tracks at the sound of that authoritative voice and turned slowly to face him, her hands clasped respectfully behind her back. She was oblivious of everything else barring the onslaught of those green eyes on her person and the blood rushed into her cheeks.

Abominable man! she thought. It was clear that he intended her to feel uncomfortable, and that was exactly how she felt under his direct scrutiny.

'What kind of work have you done prior to this?' he asked abruptly.

'I ... well, I ...' Tessa felt cornered, her life as a student and pianist flashing before her eyes like an accusation. 'I've done a bit of acting, and catering, and also secretarial work.' Thank goodness for her mother's charitable organisations, she sighed inwardly.

'I presume you have references?' he pursued the subject relentlessly.

'I—I——'

'Of course she has, Matthew,' Mrs Craig came swiftly to her rescue. 'I've seen her references and I'm quite satisfied with them.'

'Then I shall have to take your word for it, Mother,' Matthew Craig remarked thoughtfully, but it was clear that he had not yet finished with Tessa, for he pinned her down with a penetrating glance. 'Do you always find difficulty in speaking, and end up stuttering?'

Tessa pulled herself together. 'Not always.'

'Then you're obviously frightened of something,' he stated firmly, clearly arriving at some conclusion. 'Have you something to hide, Miss Smith?'

'Really, Matthew!' his mother exclaimed angrily. 'You go too far!'

'It doesn't matter, Mrs Craig,' Tessa interrupted, her anger mounting as she faced her inquisitor. 'I have nothing to hide, Mr Craig. At least, nothing that would be of interest to you.'

'Do I perhaps frighten you?'

'Not in the least.'

Mathew Craig remained silent, but his eyes stated clearly, 'liar'. Before he could say anything further, Tessa turned and fled from the room. She hurried down the passage and out on to the patio in search of fresh air and solitude, but in her haste she cannoned violently into a solid figure in the darkness.

'Whoa there! Where's the fire?'

It was Barry Craig, and Tessa could almost have cried with relief. 'I'm sorry, Mr Craig. I never noticed you in the dark.'

'I'm surprised you missed those stone pillars at the

43

speed you were travelling,' his voice teased lightly. 'What's the hurry?'

'I—I felt like going for a walk,' she explained lamely, trying to focus on the dark shape before her.

'Has Matthew been giving you a hard time?' he asked astutely.

'Not particularly, why?'

'I just wondered.' He was silent for a moment and then took hold of her arm. 'If you want to go for a walk I'd better accompany you, or you might get lost.'

'In the garden?' Tessa laughed, her jangled nerves settling into place.

'At night the garden seems to go on for ever and you might find yourself wandering aimlessly through the cane fields,' he explained, walking at a leisurely pace beside her, and for some minutes they continued their walk in silence while Tessa drew the scented air deep into her lungs.

'It's certainly peaceful here,' she remarked softly, almost hating to break the silence.

'Too peaceful at times,' Barry said bitterly. 'The silence gets you down occasionally.'

'You couldn't possibly want to exchange the peace and tranquillity of your life here with that of the mad rush in the city?'

'Wait until you've been here a month or so. The silence and monotony of life drives you insane.'

Tessa glanced curiously at the dark shape beside her. 'And you think that life in the city is never monotonous?'

'With all there is to see and do?' Barry laughed incredulously. 'You must be joking!'

'What happens when you've eventually seen and done everything?'

They continued their walk in silence while Barry chewed thoughtfully on her query. 'You come from Johannesburg, so you could answer that question yourself.'

Tessa sighed exasperatedly. 'Mr Craig——'

'Barry ... remember?'

'Very well ... Barry,' she acknowledged, smiling to herself in the darkness. 'Is the real reason for your wanting to go to the city not perhaps instigated by your desire to get away from your brother's domination?'

'You're very astute, aren't you?' he laughed briefly, his hand tightening on her arm. 'Yes, I do want to get away. Matthew says I need to learn discipline, and there are times I almost agree with him. I'm tired of taking orders from him, and it's no use arguing with him either, because in my heart I know he's right. Matthew is the sensible, solid and dependable one in our family.' There was a slight hint of bitterness in his voice. 'Matthew always knows what's good for every-one, and the terrible thing is that he's usually right. He may sound dominating but his advice is always worth taking, and there have been many occasions when I've gone against his advice simply to show that I have a mind of my own. Afterwards I've had to suffer for my stupidity, and I'm naturally thought to be irresponsible and undisciplined. I've been feeling unsettled and despondent lately, perhaps that's why the lure of the city is so enticing.'

The silence settled about them once more and Tessa

45

could not help feeling sympathetic towards the youngest member of the Craig family. He stopped suddenly and turned towards her in the darkness.

'I don't know why I've burdened you with my problems,' he said apologetically, 'but it's been good talking to you. You're a wonderful listener, Tessa Smith.'

'And I'm a stranger to you,' Tessa added quickly. 'Sometimes it's easier to talk to strangers than to someone close to you.'

'You may have a point there.'

The moon came out from behind the clouds and bathed the garden in its mysterious glow as they strolled back to the house. The light was still on in Mrs Craig's room and Tessa wondered if Matthew was still with her and, if so, what they were talking about. Was he perhaps pressing his mother for more information about her new housekeeper-companion? Tessa trembled at the thought. Perhaps she should not have accepted Mrs Craig's unusual offer of employment so readily under the circumstances.

'Are you cold?' Barry asked with quick concern, interrupting her train of thought.

'No, merely a few unpleasant thoughts,' she admitted, and hastily changed the subject. 'Have you ever thought of farming somewhere on your own?'

'I've suggested that to Matthew, but he doesn't consider me capable enough.' Barry gestured angrily with his hands. 'If only I could convince him to the contrary! Matthew and I inherited this farm together, so I suggested that he pay me out for my share so that I could buy my own piece of land, but he wouldn't hear of it.'

46

'But that's ridiculous! Surely he must realise that you would prefer to be on your own, and that you would be quite capable of making decisions for yourself?'

Barry sighed heavily. 'That's just it! I've deliberately stepped over the line on so many occasions that he just won't believe me.'

'But, if you know this, then why do you continue doing these foolish things?' Tessa asked gently.

Barry shrugged his shoulder. 'Devilment, I suppose. That's the only explanation I can offer.'

Tessa was silent for a moment as understanding dawned. 'Then you actually have only yourself to blame for your present situation.'

Barry turned to her then, his expression thoughtful in the moonlight. 'You're right, I *have* only myself to blame.'

'I do understand why, though,' Tessa whispered compassionately. 'I would also react strongly against domination, no matter how well-meant.'

Barry's spirited laughter rang out across the garden. 'You're a girl after my own heart! I think I'm going to like you, Theresa Smith.'

Tessa's heart jerked violently. 'Why did you call me Theresa?'

'Tessa is short for Theresa, isn't it?' Barry asked affably.

'Well—yes, I suppose so.' Tessa took a deep breath to control her frightened heartbeats. 'I would prefer being called Tessa, if you don't mind.'

Barry squeezed her arm. 'Very well, Tessa it is.'

To Tessa's consternation they encountered Matthew

47

on the patio. 'Mother is waiting for you to say good-night,' he told Barry abruptly, drawing deeply on his cigarette.

'I'm on my way,' Barry replied, bidding Tessa good-night with the wave of his hand.

Tessa turned swiftly to follow him indoors, but the next instant her arm was gripped tightly. 'Just a moment, Miss Smith.'

Tessa stood as if turned to stone in his grip. She was once again aware of peculiar sensations chasing along the length of her arm at his touch, but she attributed it to the fierceness of his grip.

'You're hurting me!'

He released her instantly. 'I'm sorry.'

The silence lengthened as they faced each other, and in the darkness he looked frighteningly tall, his broad shoulders blotting out the stars. The smell of after-shave lotion mingled pleasantly with that of tobacco and Tessa felt an unusual awareness take possession of her. She quivered like a frightened animal sensing danger while not knowing from which direction it would appear.

'Did you want to speak to me about something?' she asked nervously when she could bear the silence no longer.

'Yes.' Matthew Craig seemed to square his shoulders, dropping the butt of his cigarette to the ground and grinding it beneath his heel. 'I thought I'd made it clear to you that your duty lay with my mother, and not with my brother?'

Tessa bristled with anger. 'Yes, Mr Craig, you did, but I came out for a breath of fresh air and literally bumped into your brother. He insisted on walking with me and I couldn't be rude to him.' She took a deep breath and stared at the dark shape before her with a measure of defiance. 'As a matter of fact, I enjoyed his company immensely and, if asked, shall enjoy doing it again.'

'You obviously don't waste much time, do you?'

'In what way?' she asked, but she knew perfectly well what he was insinuating, and her anger merely increased.

'In becoming acquainted with members of the opposite sex.'

'Are you perhaps upset because you and I haven't had the opportunity to become acquainted?'

Tessa regretted those words instantly, for Matthew seemed to rise in stature, his attitude more chilling than the icy wind that occasionally blew down from the Drakensberg mountains.

'I have no use for women of your sort,' he said, his voice vibrating with suppressed violence.

'And what sort is that?' Tessa asked, her defiance crumbling fast.

'The sort that would sell their soul for money and possessions,' he stated harshly. 'But I warn you, you will have me to contend with.'

So Matthew Craig had branded her a gold-digger, Tessa thought in amazement, and laughter bubbled up inside her and burst past her lips. If only he knew!

'Goodnight, Mr Craig,' she managed through her laughter as she hastily walked away from him. 'Sleep well.'

Matthew Craig's muttered oath rang in her ears as

she hurried to the privacy of her room. It was only as she closed the door behind her that her laughter subsided to be replaced by an inexplicable sadness. What did it matter what he thought of her? she thought defiantly, yet strangely enough, it did matter. It was ridiculous that the opinion of someone she had met only briefly should matter so much and, despite her efforts, he dominated her thoughts for the rest of the evening.

CHAPTER THREE

TESSA spent a restless night dwelling on the events which had led to her acceptance of a job that had more or less been forced on her. In her new role as Tessa Smith it had seemed like a challenge, yet she could not help wondering whether she might not regret her decision in the future.

For some reason Matthew Craig was suspicions of her, and she could only blame this on her unorthodox arrival. If she had actually been Miss Emmerson's replacement, she would have displayed more confidence and the necessary references to confirm her reliability, instead of which she was vague in her replies to queries and entirely unbusinesslike. Matthew might forgive this form of deceit, but would he forgive her assumed identity?

Tessa was up and dressed by five-thirty and, trying not to disturb the others, she went through to the kitchen to start the fire in order to make some coffee. Fifteen minutes later she was still struggling with the reluctant stove. Her patience at the end of its tether, she repacked the fire and struck another match without success, and merely succeeded in burning her fingers.

'Oh, damn!' she swore softly to herself, sucking at her fingers and inspecting the damage.

'Having problems?'

Tessa shot upright at the sound of that voice, her heart jolting violently as she saw Matthew Craig leaning against the side of the door, his arms folded across his chest, and his glance decidedly mocking. She ran the tip of her tongue across her dry lips and admitted defeat.

'The fire won't burn.'

Matthew Craig's glance seemed to scorch her and, to her chagrin, she felt her cheeks grow hot. How she hated this man's arrogance and self-assurance.

'Perhaps I can help you,' he observed as he came towards her, but Tessa was not fooled. He was deriving immense satisfaction from the whole situation by proving her incapable, and Tessa could not argue away her inability to light the fire. He glanced about the smoke-filled kitchen and summed up the situation instantly. 'If you open the damper the fire will burn without any problems. It causes the necessary draught to kindle the fire, and once it's burning properly you can close the the damper or leave it slightly open to regulate the temperature of the oven.'

'Oh.' Tessa felt foolish as she watched him set to work.

He finally struck a match, cupped it for a moment in his well-shaped hands, and lit the fire. As the flames rose higher, he straightened and glanced down at her, apparently amused at her discomfort. 'It's easy when you know how, isn't it?'

Tessa bit back a sharp retort and met his glance unwaveringly. He had made his point. 'Thank you for your help, Mr Craig. I'm sorry I had to trouble you.'

'It was no trouble,' he remarked casually. 'I merely wanted to make sure I would have something to drink before I went into the fields.'

Tessa was seething with anger as he turned to leave, her eyes looking daggers at his back. In the doorway he paused and turned.

'By the way, there's a black smudge on your nose,' he remarked before disappearing down the passage.

Tessa's hand went instantly to her nose and came away with the tell-tale smudge on the tips of her fingers. 'Bother the man!' she thought as she rubbed her nose vigorously with her handkerchief. Why did he have to make her feel such a fool?

She hastily filled the kettle and placed it on the polished black surface of the stove. The fire was now burning lustily and while she waited for the kettle to boil she set out the cups and hunted for the coffee. She wondered idly what her parents would say if they could see her at that moment. Her mother would naturally be concerned and upset, while her father would find it all an enormous joke. She would have to write to them soon to tell them her address or they might think she was still roaming about the countryside. She laughed softly to herself. She had certainly not planned this part of her trip, and never expected that she would find herself employed without even applying.

'Something amuses you?'

Tessa's expression sobered instantly. Matthew had returned without making a sound and she tensed instantly as he pulled out a chair and sat down. She had not noticed earlier how attractive he looked in his khaki slacks and shirt with his skin tanned from the hours spent in the sun, and his fair hair slightly dampened and combed back from his forehead. Most of the men she knew wore their hair slightly long, according to the modern trend, but this man's hair was trimmed neatly at the sides and back of his well-shaped head. Her father would approve of Matthew Craig, she thought. He was, according to Barry, sensible and dependable, two qualities her father always admired in someone. She drew her breath in sharply. What was she thinking!

Matthew's green eyes were regarding her questioningly and, realising that she had been staring, she hastily averted her face to hide her crimson cheeks, and poured him a cup of coffee.

'I asked if something amused you,' he persisted as she placed his coffee in front of him on the table.

'I'm not easily amused, Mr Craig,' Tessa replied, setting out a tray for Mrs Craig.

'Really?' He sipped at his coffee thoughtfully. 'Something I said last night apparently succeeded in amusing you.'

Tessa's heart was thudding heavily against her ribs. 'You wouldn't understand.'

Matthew Craig reminded her of a leopard preparing to attack its prey and she shrank from him mentally, thankful that she had something with which to keep her hands occupied.

'If you feel you have something to confide, I can assure you that I'm a good listener.'

There was a steel-like quality about this man that frightened her, and she hated to think what he would do if he should ever discover her deception.

'I have nothing to confide,' she replied coldly, her throat tightening with nervous tension. 'And if ever the necessity arose to do so, then I certainly shouldn't choose you as my confidant.'

Matthew's expression hardened visibly, his eyes glinting dangerously. 'You may yet have to confide in me, Tessa Smith, and when you do ...' his lips tightened, 'I shall not be lenient with you.'

Tessa escaped to Mrs Craig's room with the tray of coffee. To have had to stay in the kitchen with Matthew one minute longer, was unbearable, and she was seriously thinking of asking Mrs Craig to release her instantly. 'Coward', her conscience jeered.

'You seem upset, Tessa,' Ethel Craig remarked as Tessa sat down beside her while she drank her coffee. 'Has something happened?'

Tessa's frown deepened. 'Mrs Craig, I don't think it was such a good idea employing me. I'm not really qualified for this sort of thing.'

'What nonsense!' her employer protested. 'Surely I am the one who should judge your capabilities?'

'That's just it!' Tessa exclaimed. 'I've offered you no reference by which to judge. What do you really know of me? How do you know that I shan't exploit your faith in me?'

Ethel Craig gazed intently at her with a curious light in her eyes which puzzled her. 'I trust you implicitly, Tessa.'

Those words, so quietly and sincerely spoken, brought a lump to Tessa's throat. 'Mrs Craig, if you should discover that I have ... lied to you, what would you say?'

'Then I would say that you had a very good reason for doing so,' the older woman replied without hesitation.

A shuddering sigh escaped Tessa's lips. 'Mrs Craig, your son Matthew doesn't like me very much, that's why I thought it would be best if he found someone else ... someone more capable.'

'Matthew is always a little difficult with strangers until he gets to know them,' Mrs Craig admitted laughingly. 'Give him time to adjust to your presence, my dear.'

'I don't think we shall ever get to know each other,' Tessa remarked dubiously. 'On the few occasions we've met, since my arrival yesterday, we've come close to openly declaring war.'

Mrs Craig chuckled to herself as she placed her empty cup on the tray. 'If you should leave my employ, as you've suggested, you'll be admitting defeat and playing right into Matthew's hands.'

This was a challenge, something which Tessa had never been able to resist. If there was going to be open warfare between Matthew Craig and herself, then she at least had his mother's permission to indulge in it.

Matthew returned some time later to have breakfast, but he was silent as Tessa served him and Barry in the dining-room. Mrs Craig preferred having a tray sent to her room so that Tessa could have more time to help her dress after the breakfast had been seen to. Lunch and dinner they normally had together in the dining-room, Mrs Craig had told her, although Matthew often skipped lunch if he was busy with something.

Barry strolled into the kitchen later that morning and Tessa glanced nervously beyond him to see if Matthew would follow.

'Don't worry, I'm alone,' he grinned mischievously, somehow sensing her anxiety. 'Am I in time for tea?'

'Yes,' Tessa laughed nervously. 'I'm just waiting for the kettle to boil.' She pushed a plate of biscuits towards him. 'Sit down and try one of these while you're waiting.'

Barry helped himself and bit into the freshly baked biscuit. 'Hmm ... did you make these?'

'Yes ... with Daisy's help, of course. She's an absolute marvel at explaining things.' Daisy's dark face glowed at this unexpected compliment from Tessa.

'They're delicious,' was Barry's verdict. 'Could I have another one?'

'You may,' Tessa smiled, removing the last batch of biscuits from the oven.

'Where did you learn to cook like this?'

'At home we——' Tessa stopped herself in time. She had been on the verge of divulging the fact that they had a chef at home who had always been willing to impart with his knowledge, and this statement alone would have evoked awkward questions. 'At home we've always been fond of cooking, and this was merely an experiment,' she concluded lamely.

'Then please continue experimenting,' Barry grinned at her. 'Where's Mother?'

'In the living-room, writing letters.' Tessa stood about uncomfortably. 'You wouldn't perhaps like to go through and keep her company while I'm making the tea?'

Barry's glance was slightly mocking. 'Are you trying to get rid of me?'

'No, but Matthew wouldn't like it if he found you sitting here in the kitchen chatting to me.'

Tessa felt ridiculously like a child who was trespassing. Matthew Craig had instructed that she should 'keep off' where Barry was concerned and, despite the fact that she had determined not to pay attention to this, she could not prevent herself from feeling that she was deliberately disobeying orders. Oh, how she hated Matthew Craig's superior attitude!

'He's suspicious of you, did you know that?' Barry interrupted her thoughts and Tessa glanced at him sharply. 'He says you haven't the hands of an ordinary working class girl, and you own a Porsche which is last year's model. Matthew says that no hard-working girl could afford a car like that unless . . .'

'Unless what?' Tessa demanded, noticing a faint redness seeping into his face. 'Well, go on, you might as well tell me the worst.'

Barry helped himself to another biscuit and bit into it self-consciously. 'Unless you acquired it for services rendered . . . if you know what I mean?'

Tessa's breath caught in her throat as she faced Barry across the kitchen. The blood surged into her cheeks and then receded, leaving her deathly pale. 'Is that what he thinks?'

The implication behind Barry's words had been all too clear. Matthew saw her as a girl with a reputation which was unsavoury, and if she had judged him correctly, he would endeavour to prove that his supposition was correct. Tessa shuddered at the thought. Not for the first time did she curse herself for stopping to ask the way, for her innocent decision had landed her in a situation which could very easily become embarrassing.

'I didn't say that Matthew thought *that* of you, but

merely that it was a supposition,' Barry continued, trying to save the situation. 'As a matter of interest, where *did* you get that car?'

A flicker of amusement crossed her sensitive face. 'It was a gift from two very dear people ... with no strings attached.'

'Were you employed by them?'

'No.'

'Then how——'

'No more questions, please,' Tessa interrupted, turning away as the kettle boiled over on the stove.

'You're a mystery, Tessa Smith, and mysteries have always intrigued me,' Barry remarked, the chair scraping on the wooden floor as he got to his feet.

'Don't let your imagination run away with you, Barry,' she advised him seriously. 'I'm just an ... ordinary girl, trying to do my job as best I can.'

From the living-room window one had a magnificent view down into the valley, beyond which the plantations stretched as far as the eye could see, transforming the gently rolling hills into a living, breathing thing as the sugar cane swayed in the breeze. In the garden below the hibiscus, poinsettia and bougainvillaea were flowering, their colours brilliant in the sunshine and dazzling to Tessa's eyes.

It had been a peaceful morning despite Barry's disturbing news, and Tessa remained in the living-room with Mrs Craig long after he had left them. She could perhaps not blame Matthew entirely for speculating about her character, for she had practically appeared from nowhere to take up a position in his home which had not been intended for her. The slight deception his mother had forced her into was nothing compared to the deception she was carrying out, and she shuddered to think what Matthew's reaction would be if he discovered the truth. No, she decided eventually, it would be far better to suffer his insults than to feel the sting of his wrath. No one took kindly to being deceived, and Matthew Craig would be no exception, for he was essentially a proud man, and an honest one.

'Good morning, Mother.'

Tessa's nerves received a violent jolt as the object of her thoughts entered the living-room. He inclined his head slightly in her direction and proceeded to take no further notice of her. For some unknown reason, his attitude had the power to hurt her, and she was even more surprised to discover that she would far rather have him for a friend than an enemy. It was absolutely ridiculous to feel this way about someone she hardly knew, she told herself angrily, but Matthew Craig, in the short time she had known him, presented a challenge to her which she could not ignore so lightly.

'I have to go to Idwala this afternoon,' he said quietly, drawing a chair nearer to his mother's and sitting down. 'Is there perhaps anything I could get for you?'

Ethel Craig was thoughtful for a moment. 'I have only these few letters to be posted,' she said, gesturing to the sealed envelopes on the table beside her. 'There *is* something you could do for me, my dear. You could take Tessa along with you so that she can become acquainted with our town, small though it is.'

Matthew raised his eyebrows and looked as though

he was about to refuse when Tessa forestalled him. 'Oh, please, Mrs Craig!' she said quickly. 'I'm sure Mr Craig wouldn't like the idea of my tagging along.'

'Nonsense!' Ethel Craig retorted, her glance sweeping her son. 'Matthew won't mind at all. Will you, Matthew?'

'Well, I——'

'There's this evening's dinner to be seen to,' Tessa forestalled him once again, biting her lip nervously. 'I can't possibly go out.'

'Daisy can manage perfectly well until your return,' Ethel insisted adamantly. 'You could post my letters for me. Running errands is, after all, part of a house-keeper-companion's job,' she added with a humorous twinkle in her eyes at Tessa's reluctance.

'When you put it like that, I suppose I shall have to do as you say,' Tessa agreed with a sigh as she faced Matthew, noticing his lips tighten in a way that chilled her.

'I shall be leaving immediately after lunch,' he said abruptly, getting to his feet and towering above her. 'Be ready, and don't keep me waiting.'

Without another word he turned on his heel and left the room. The silence was tense for a moment as Ethel frowned at the floor, while Tessa shifted uncomfortably in her chair.

'I don't know what's come over Matthew,' Ethel remarked with some confusion. 'He's being extremely rude, and unnecessarily so, I feel. I must apologise, Tessa, but I can assure you that he isn't normally like this.' She shook her grey head. 'I wonder if something is troubling him?'

Tessa could have told her without much effort what

was troubling her son, instead she instantly reassured her. 'Please don't let his attitude towards me trouble you. He's naturally cautious, and you should be grateful for this.'

'That's no excuse for being rude,' Ethel persisted, unusually perturbed. 'I've never known him like this.'

'Mrs Craig ...' Tessa began hesitantly, her throat tightening with nervousness. 'What will he do if he should discover that I was not sent as a replacement for Miss Emmerson, and that I——?'

'He'll be furious, naturally,' Ethel interrupted without hesitation, a smile tugging at her lips. 'I shall, of course, tell him after you've left, and I'm certain that he will understand how I dreaded the whole business of interviewing prospective employees once more.'

Tessa could only stare at her employer and shake her head helplessly, wishing that, when the moment of truth arrived, she could be a fly on the wall to witness Matthew's reaction. It should be amusing, she decided eventually.

Matthew was morosely silent as they drove to Idwala that afternoon, and the dreadful part was that Tessa could think of absolutely nothing to say to break the uncomfortable silence between them. It was a pity, she decided, that Matthew could not accept her presence in his home as easily as Barry had done. It would have made her stay so much more pleasant, she thought unhappily.

During the few minutes she had had to spare before lunch, she had written a short letter to her parents informing them of the peculiar situation she had become involved in, stressing the fact that if they should write to her, they should use her newly acquired name of Tessa Smith. She had carefully avoided mentioning Matthew's attitude towards her, and painted the picture as rosy as possible for their peace of mind. Tessa kept this letter carefully hidden in her handbag, and hoped fervently that Matthew would not accompany her to the post office counter. The name and address on the envelope would merely increase his curiosity and place her in an even worse predicament than she already was.

She glanced at Matthew surreptitiously, acutely conscious of his presence beside her. His attractive face was expressionless and his eyes never wavered from the road ahead. What was he thinking? she wondered curiously as she stole another glance at him. There were laughter lines around his eyes, yet, strangely enough, she had not yet seen him laughing.

He must have sensed that he was being observed, for he glanced at her quickly before returning his eyes to the road. Tessa averted her glance hastily and fiddled nervously with the clasp of her handbag.

'I must apologise for the fact that I was more or less forced upon you this afternoon,' she interrupted the silence, swallowing nervously at the lump in her throat.

'One good thing will result from this excursion,' he said abruptly, not sparing her feelings. 'Now that you know the way, you'll be able to drive to Idwala on your own.'

'Please don't think I'm enjoying this trip,' she was stung to retort. 'I'm hating every minute of it as much as you are, and I wouldn't dream of making a habit of it.'

'It's a relief to know that you feel that way about it,'

he concluded the conversation, but Tessa was not prepared to leave it there.

'Why do you hate me so much, Mr Craig?' she asked.

'I don't hate you,' he replied, raising his eyebrows mockingly. 'I neither hate you nor like you. It's as simple as that.'

'Then why are you so rude to me?' she persisted, determined to bring about some sort of truce between them.

'If I'm rude, then I must apologise,' Matthew remarked dryly. 'It appears as though my attitude has upset you, or is it that you're so used to men falling over themselves to receive your favours that my attitude of uninterest displeases you?'

'That was uncalled for,' Tessa whispered, striving to keep calm despite the fact that she was trembling with anger. 'I merely wish to convey to you the fact that your rudeness towards me upsets your mother, and despite the fact that we dislike each other so much, I was hoping that we could make some sort of pretence at civility in her presence.'

Matthew turned the car off the road and applied the brakes. 'What manner of civility did you have in mind?' he asked mockingly, reaching for her.

'Certainly not the kind you have in mind!' Tessa exclaimed hotly, retreating into the furthest corner in an effort to evade his arms.

'You disappoint me, Tessa Smith,' he remarked, regarding her closely. 'What kind of civility did you have in mind, then?'

Tessa was unnerved by his nearness and close scrutiny. 'I—I would like us to call a truce for the duration

64

of my stay ... which will last only six weeks until your mother is on her feet once more.'

Matthew regarded her steadily and she could have sworn there was a flicker of amusement in his green eyes before his expression hardened. For some reason he frightened her, and she trembled with relief as he turned away from her and pressed the starter.

'We'll call a truce, you and I,' he agreed as he released the clutch and allowed the Mercedes to speed forward, 'but this doesn't mean that I'm entirely satisfied with you, Miss Smith.'

Tessa decided wisely that it would be futile to pursue the subject further. They had temporarily called a truce and that was what she had been aiming at.

Idwala was not a large town by the usual standards, and she was thankful when Matthew left her to her own devices after parking the car and instructing her to meet him in the parking lot within an hour. He directed her to the post office, but did not accompany her as she went inside, after which she walked about exploring the shops. She bought a few magazines to take back with her and, after glancing at her wristwatch, decided to return to the car to wait for Matthew rather than have him wait for her.

So engrossed was she in one of her magazines that she did not see nor hear him approach, and only became aware of his presence when he spoke beside her. 'Would you like to come and have a cup of tea with me before we leave?'

The unexpectedness of the invitation left her speechless for a moment, and she saw the all too familiar frown of annoyance creasing his brow.

'If you would rather not, then I shall understand,' he said abruptly. 'I merely thought we could celebrate our truce with a cup of tea.'

'That would be lovely,' Tessa said quickly, not wishing to add to his annoyance by hesitating further.

Matthew helped her from the car and took her arm. She was very conscious of his hand against her skin as he guided her across the street towards the café, and she felt her pulse quickening as that now familiar sensation quivered along her nervous system. The interior of the café was cool and Matthew selected a table close to the entrance.

'You seem surprised that I should have asked you to have tea with me,' he remarked after he had placed their order.

'I am,' Tessa admitted truthfully, a nervous little smile fluttering about her lips. It was a rather terrifying experience for her to be seated opposite him with only the narrow breadth of the small table between them, and she was not at all sure of his reason for inviting her there.

'Correct me if I'm wrong,' he continued smoothly, 'but you were the one who suggested we should call a truce. Is that not so?'

'Yes, but——'

'Do you wish to withdraw it?'

'No!' her breath caught in her throat. 'No, I don't! I merely didn't expect you to accept my suggestion so readily.'

His lips twisted into a semblance of a smile, but their tea was served to them at that moment and their conversation was discontinued. Tessa poured their tea in silence with a hand that was not quite steady, and she sensed that Matthew was not unaware of her nervousness, for his probing eyes missed very little.

'Tell me, Miss Smith,' he said after a while, 'when most young girls have permanent employment these days, why do you prefer to take jobs of this nature which only last for a short period? Do you perhaps object to the stability of anything permanent?'

Tessa raised her head sharply and gazed at him with startled eyes. 'Not—not at all,' she stammered, momentarily confused. 'Shall we say that I have a restless nature?'

Matthew gazed at her intently with narrowed eyes and Tessa felt a shiver of apprehension go through her. This was a man who was not easily deceived and, from the way he questioned her, she knew that he would not rest until he had discovered the entire truth. 'And then, Tessa Smith,' she told herself ruefully, 'your carefully contrived experiment will have failed miserably.'

'I have a peculiar feeling that for some reason you're not telling me the truth.' He leaned towards her, his green eyes glittering dangerously. 'I hope I'm wrong?'

Tessa felt as though a giant hand had taken possession of her chest and was squeezing every ounce of breath from her body. What could she say to allay his suspicions? If she told him the truth, her desire for anonymity—the desire to be accepted for herself—would have been futile. To guard her secret she would have to revert back to lies which were becoming increasingly unpalatable.

She sighed heavily and pushed agitated fingers through her short curls. 'Mr Craig, won't you please try to accept me as I am?' Her blue eyes were pleading with him in all sincerity. 'I'm here to assist your mother, and I shall do my best for her—that I can promise you.'

'I wonder,' he murmured softly, his eyes never leaving her face. 'There's something about you that doesn't quite ring true, but for the moment I can't seem to put my finger on it.' A determined look crossed his lean features which disturbed her immensely. 'Nevertheless, it will come to me eventually, I'm sure.'

Tessa could not recall entirely what had transpired during the journey home that afternoon. She knew only that she was conscious of his disturbing presence beside her, and of the mad desire to escape before it was too late. Her thoughts were not explicit at that moment and she wondered confusedly from which she desired to escape the most ... from Matthew's wrath before he discovered her true identity ... or from Matthew Craig as a person, and the effect he had upon her emotions?

'There is just one other matter I wish to discuss with you,' he said grimly before they parted company. 'Your refusal to have your meals with the family.'

'I would prefer——'

'What you would prefer doesn't concern me,' he interrupted brusquely, brushing aside her protestations. 'In future you have your meals with the family—and that's an order!'

CHAPTER FOUR

TESSA'S fears were lulled into semi-obscurity during the next few days. Since she and Matthew had called a tentative truce, they actually managed to be pleasant towards each other, and if he still harboured suspicions about her, he gave no indication of this whenever they were together. She knew that she was basking in false security, but her deepening friendship with Mrs Craig and her two sons was something she did not want to relinquish, or mar with troubled thoughts.

The harvesting season had begun for the cane farmers and Tessa found herself alone most of the day with Mrs Craig. Matthew and Barry were in the plantations supervising the harvesting and seldom returned home before sunset. After dinner in the evenings Barry often went out, while Matthew withdrew to his study. On a few occasions Tessa had taken him a cup of coffee during the evening, and as a result of this he had politely asked her to join him. At first she had been terribly nervous, then gradually she began to relax in his company when it became clear to her that he had no intention of asking further personal or awkward questions. On one occasion only had he come close to being personal, and Tessa remembered it vividly. She had bought herself several loose-fitting overalls to wear over her clothes, and this obviously displeased Matthew.

'Do you have to wear those drab overalls all the time?' he had asked. 'They have no shape whatsoever, and make you look dowdy.'

'I—I have to wear them,' she had stammered nervously, fiddling with the top button. 'They save my clothes tremendously.'

'I would prefer to see you without them,' he had said, coming towards her with a curious look in his eyes. 'You have an enchanting figure. Why hide it beneath this shapeless overall?'

Her heartbeats had quickened, and she stood paralysed as he unbuttoned her overall and slid it off her shoulders to reveal a plain woollen dress that clung more closely to her figure. Matthew dropped the overall on to a chair as his glance slid over her. Tessa had trembled beneath his gaze, her cheeks pink with embarrassment.

'In something more stylish you would be very attractive,' he said, and his gaze lingered. '*Very* attractive *indeed*.'

He was so close to her that she could feel his cool breath against her forehead, and an inexplicable longing to feel the strength of his arms about her took possession of her. This longing was swiftly replaced by wild panic. Tessa snatched up her overall and hastily excused herself. Further along the passage she had stopped to place her hands against her burning cheeks, and wished her heart would resume its steady pace. What was the matter with her? she had wondered frantically. No man had ever affected her in this way before, but then Matthew was no ordinary man. He was ...

She drew her breath in sharply and refused to linger on the subject.

Barry went to Idwala one morning to collect the post and returned with a letter for Tessa. It was from her parents, she realised as she recognised her mother's handwriting on the envelope, and she hastily pushed it into her overall pocket.

Barry raised his eyebrows speculatively as he watched her, and remarked teasingly, 'Is it a letter from your boy-friend?'

'What makes you think that?' she asked innocently.

'Just a hunch,' Barry shrugged knowingly.

Tessa did not disillusion him and merely smiled secretively as she continued rolling out the pastry for the apple pie. Barry stood about for a moment longer, but when it became apparent that Tessa was not in the mood for conversation, he slouched off towards the living-room where Tessa knew Mrs Craig would be sitting in front of the large French windows looking out on to the garden.

She did not have an opportunity to read her letter until after lunch that day when she could safely go to her room without being disturbed. She had been away from home for three weeks and knew a great longing to hear from the two people most dear to her.

'Dear Tessa,' her mother had written in her small, neat handwriting, 'we were horrified to learn of what you are doing and at the same time, relieved to know that you are not traipsing about the country as we thought.

'Your father has asked me to issue a word of warning: Deceiving people whom you meet only casually is one thing, but deceiving those with whom you are in close contact daily could be disastrous. I'm afraid that on this occasion I must agree with him. No one likes to be the victim of deceit, however innocent the reason for the deception.

'Jeremy telephoned and asked after you. After more than a year he was suddenly concerned about you, but I think I managed to reassure him. I was very tempted to give him a piece of my mind when I realised that perhaps it had all happened for the best. Marriage can never be a one-sided affair, my dear, and Jeremy fortunately realised this in time.

'Let us know how soon we can expect you home, but in the mean time take care of yourself and write soon. Your loving parents.'

Tessa lowered the letter slowly and stared through her window to where the cane fields stretched across the hills. Jeremy! There was no longer that leaden feeling in her breast at the mention of his name and, strangely enough, she hardly ever thought of him any more. She had loved Jeremy once, as much as she had thought she could ever love anyone, and to discover that he had deceived her had been a blow from which she had thought she would never recover, and yet ... the pain and the longing had diminished, leaving only that terrible doubt which had instigated this mad desire to be accepted for herself.

Tessa was brought back sharply to the present by the sound of Mrs Craig's bell ringing, and she hid the letter beneath her clothes in the drawer. She would have to destroy it later when she had had the opportunity to read it once more, she decided as she left her room, closing the door firmly behind her.

She was busy in the kitchen after dinner that evening when the telephone rang shrilly in the hall and swiftly she went to answer it.

'Hello?' a woman's melodious voice said. 'Is that Mrs Craig's housekeeper?'

'That's putting me in my place,' Tessa thought wryly before replying, 'Yes, that's right.'

'Miss ... er ... Smith, I believe?' the voice at the other end persisted.

Why did everyone always hesitate over the name "Smith"? 'Yes.'

'I'm Angela Sinclair,' the woman introduced herself, pausing slightly. 'I suppose you've heard of me?'

'I'm afraid I haven't,' Tessa replied truthfully.

'Oh ... is Matthew around somewhere?' Angela Sinclair, whoever she was, sounded slightly deflated.

'I'll ask him to come to the telephone,' Tessa said briskly. Moments later she was knocking on the door to Matthew's study.

'Yes?' she heard him call before she opened the door.

'Miss Angela Sinclair is on the telephone,' she told him, taking in the papers strewn all over his desk.

'Thank you,' he frowned, dropping his pen on to the desk and following her down the dimly lit passage.

Tessa hurried back to the kitchen, but could nevertheless hear every word he spoke on the telephone even though he hardly raised his voice.

'Hello, Angela,' she heard him say. 'No, not particu-

larly ... yes, all right, I'll be there as soon as I can ...
'Bye.'

He replaced the receiver and Tessa could hear his footsteps echoing down the passage towards his bedroom. A sigh escaped her and for some inexplicable reason she felt as though the world was weighing heavily upon her shoulders. She pulled herself together instantly and concentrated on the list before her, but the lilting voice of Angela Sinclair kept ringing in her ears. She obviously meant a great deal to Matthew that he could drop whatever he was doing to go to her the moment she called!

'What's keeping you in the kitchen so late this evening?'

Tessa glanced up swiftly to see him dwarfing the doorway. She had been so lost in thought that she had not heard him return, and his unexpected presence in the kitchen unnerved her for some reason.

'I shall have to go and do some grocery shopping for your mother tomorrow,' she said quickly, unable to meet his penetrating glance. 'I'm checking through everything and making a list of what's required.'

He came towards her and stood beside her at the table, so close in fact that she could have touched him with only the slightest movement. This irrational thought sent a pulse jerking uncomfortably in her throat.

'If Mother should wonder where I am,' she heard him say from somewhere above her head, 'tell her I've gone to Idwala to see Angela, will you?'

'Yes, I'll do that,' she replied stiffly.

Matthew moved away from her and then in the doorway he lifted his hand. 'Au revoir.'

His footsteps disappeared down the short passage. The front door opened and closed and moments later she heard the Mercedes being driven away. A desperate longing took possession of her. There was only one way she could find relief for her pent-up emotions and that was at the piano, where her innermost feelings could flow from her fingers and into the music. She wondered nervously if Mrs Craig would be awakened by her playing, and decided to take a quick look whether her employer was asleep. To her dismay she discovered that Mrs Craig was still awake.

'Was that the telephone I heard a short while ago?' she asked as Tessa quietly entered her room.

'Yes, Mrs Craig.' Tessa walked across to the bed, her footsteps muffled by the thick carpets. 'Did it wake you?'

'No, I've been lying here reading,' Ethel Craig replied, removing her spectacles and closing her book. 'Who telephoned?'

'A Miss Sinclair. She wanted to speak to Matthew.'

'Angela?'

'Yes,' Tessa nodded, straightening the bedclothes. 'Matthew asked me to tell you that he's gone to Idwala to see her.'

'Oh ... she's a lovely girl,' the older woman smiled. 'I do wish Matthew would make up his mind about her. They've been seeing quite a lot of each other over the past two years, but Matthew seems to be in no hurry to make the relationship permanent.' Ethel Craig sighed heavily. 'It would be such a shame if someone were to whisk her off from right under his nose.'

'Yes, I'm sure it will be,' Tessa agreed, an uncommon tightness in her throat.

'Is Barry out as well?'

'Yes, he's playing chess with one of his friends.'

'Rather inconsiderate of my two sons to leave us so entirely alone here on the farm, don't you think?' Ethel remarked, gesturing that Tessa should sit down beside her on the bed.

'There's no danger, surely?' Tessa asked quickly as she subsided on to the bed and imprisoned one of her employer's slender hands between her own.

'Not with old Madala and his sons patrolling the grounds,' Ethel reassured confidently.

'Do they really?' Tessa asked in surprise. She had never thought that there would be any necessity to guard the house and the grounds.

'Ever since that night the old house burnt down, they've made it a ritual to patrol the grounds. There was talk, you see, that the fire was deliberately started by two labourers whom Matthew had ordered off the farm.'

'Were they ever caught?'

'No,' Ethel shook her head, the lamplight turning her grey hair to silver, 'and if they *did* start the fire, then they apparently decided they'd done enough damage.'

'How dreadful!' Tessa exclaimed, mulling over the thought that this terrifying incident might occur once more.

'Yes, it was dreadful,' Ethel admitted, 'but let's talk no more about it.' Her glance sharpened with concern. 'Tessa, you look indescribably sad this evening. Is there something troubling you?'

Tessa patted Mrs Craig's hand reassuringly. 'It's nothing you need be concerned about.'

76

'But I *am* concerned, my dear,' Ethel insisted, struggling into a sitting position. 'Can't you tell me what it is?'

Tessa lowered her dark head and swallowed with difficulty. 'Mrs Craig, you're very kind,' she managed, her voice no more than a whisper, 'but there's really nothing—nothing I ...'

'You *are* happy here, Tessa?'

'Oh, yes!'

'Matthew is no longer being difficult, is he?' Ethel persisted anxiously with her questioning.

'No.' Tessa raised her head and laughed slightly. 'Not since we called a truce.'

'I'm happy to hear that,' Ethel sighed, relaxing against the pillows, and closing her eyes for a moment.

During the ensuing silence Tessa plucked up the courage to ask the question which was foremost in her mind. 'Mrs Craig, would it disturb you if I played the piano a little this evening?'

Ethel Craig's eyes widened in astonishment. 'Not at all, Tessa. If I'd known that you could play I would have asked you to do so long ago. It would be lovely to have music in the house again now that Matthew seems so preoccupied with the farm.'

'I had no idea Matthew could play.' A strange excitement swept through Tessa.

Ethel smiled sadly. 'He used to play quite often, but lately he seems to have lost interest.'

'Well ... if you're sure that ...'

'My dear, please feel free to play whenever you wish,' Ethel assured her. 'I certainly shan't object.'

'Thank you, Mrs Craig,' Tessa smiled at her thankfully, and impulsively she leaned over and kissed the

77

older woman on the cheek. 'Goodnight'

'Goodnight, Tessa.'

The night was all at once oppressively silent as Tessa entered the living-room and walked hesitantly across to the upright piano at the other end of the room. How long it had been since she last played, she thought as she lifted the lid and lightly caressed the keys, then she sat down on the stool and gently pressed a few chords before lapsing into a melody. Her supple, practised fingers moved over the keyboard with assurance, and suddenly the living-room was filled with music that was both nostalgic as well as being exquisitely rendered.

Tessa could not remember how long she sat there playing, but the music flowed from her fingertips while every vestige of emotion within her breast seemed to surge into the music. She knew that she was playing with her heart and, as on so many other occasions, she realised what her professor had meant when he had tried to explain how a piece should be played.

'With the heart and not with the head,' he had stormed at her, not sparing her feelings. 'Don't just press the notes down as though you were a robot pushing down buttons. Caress the keys, or pound them with the feelings of the heart. You must speak from the heart through the music to make it laugh or cry. Remember that!'

Tonight the music was crying. The sadness in her heart was spilling out into the melody until it laughed at her with gentle mockery, and it brought relief as she gave herself in complete surrender. It was only as the last notes died away that she became aware of the peculiar sensation that she was not alone. She turned slowly on the stool to see Matthew reclining in one of the armchairs.

'How long have you been there?' she whispered nervously, closing the piano lid and getting to her feet.

'Long enough,' he replied, rising as well and walking slowly towards her. 'Why did you stop?'

Matthew's expression was unfathomable as she faced him. 'I—It's late,' she stammered confusedly, endeavouring to pass him. 'Goodnight, Mr Craig.'

'Just a minute!' She found her wrist imprisoned firmly in his grasp. 'Where did you learn to play like that?'

'I took piano lessons,' she replied tonelessly, struggling to free herself and finally succeeding.

'Who was your teacher?' he rapped the next question at her.

'Why do you want to know?' Tessa had a premonition that Matthew was trying to trap her and, making a desperate effort, she gathered her scattered wits about her.

'Don't answer my question with another,' Matthew snapped, visibly agitated. 'Who was your teacher?'

Tessa searched her memory frantically to recall the name of her very first music teacher who would, after so many years, surely not remember with clarity all the names of her pupils. 'Mrs Doyle of Johannesburg.'

Matthew's eyes darkened. 'And who else?'

Tessa made an effort to pass him once more. 'Please, Mr Craig, it's late and I——'

'Tessa,' he said sharply, gripping her shoulders and forcing her to face him, 'you didn't merely have piano

79

lessons as a child. You play too well for that.'

His hands were burning her skin through the thin material of her blouse and her pulse rate quickened alarmingly. 'You—you appear to know a lot about music?' she managed to ask.

'Enough to know that you were taught by a master. Let me see your hands,' he ordered, releasing her shoulders and catching hold of her hands where they hung limply at her sides. He examined them closely, paying particular attention to her strong, supple fingers with their tell-tale flat tips. They were a pianist's hands, her professor had always told her, and Matthew, if he knew as much as she suspected, would notice this, she realised with alarm. 'Did you study music at university?'

'No! she cried in alarm at the suddenness of the question. 'Oh, why do you persist in questioning me like this?' She was frighteningly close to tears, but Matthew was relentless in his search for the truth.

'If I'm persistent in my questioning,' he continued' without releasing her, 'it's because you play with mastery; with warmth and depth and feeling, which is something you wouldn't learn by merely plodding through your music exams in the ordinary way.' He pulled her closer to him, so close, in fact, that she could feel the heat of his body against her own. 'Who *are* you, Tessa?'

'What do you mean, who am I?' she asked unsteadily, a nerve throbbing at the base of her throat.

'Just exactly that! Who are you?'

'That's a ridiculous question,' she reprimanded him with a last gesture of defiance. 'You know who I am.'

'I know who you *say* you are,' he agreed harshly, and then, surprisingly, he released her. Tessa stood waiting, her body tense and fraught with nerves. 'All right, Tessa, relax,' he sighed, pushing his hands through his hair in an agitated fashion. 'I start off by asking you an innocent question and it almost ends up in a full-scale row.' He took her chin between his strong fingers and forced her to meet his glance. 'Why do you have to be so cagey about yourself?'

There was a look in his eyes which she could not define. His nearness disturbed her and she hid her treacherous emotions behind a slight display of anger.

'I'm *not* being cagey, but if I have no wish to divulge any personal information about myself, then why must you persist in questioning me the way you do?'

'Tessa, answer me just one more question, and if you answer it truthfully, I shan't ever pester you again with questions. Will you do that?'

His green eyes held hers captive and she felt herself weakening despite the certain knowledge that he could trap her quite easily at that moment if he should try. 'I—I'll try,' she stammered warily.

'Being a housekeeper is not your true profession, is it?'

Tessa drew her breath in slowly through parted lips. 'No.'

There was a look of triumph in his eyes as if she had confessed to something which he had already known. 'I'm afraid your negative answer leads me to just one final question.' Tessa waited with bated breath. 'Whom, or what, are you hiding from?'

The tension released its vice-like grip on her. 'You could say I'm hiding from myself.'

Matthew's eyebrows rose sharply. 'How on earth am I supposed to interpret that remark?'

'Interpet it in whatever way you like,' she replied, turning away from him and biting her lip. 'There's one more statement I could add, though. I'm not a criminal on the run from the police.'

'I know that.'

Tessa swung round sharply, her heart missing a beat. 'Have you been checking up at the local police station to discover whether I have a record?'

'No.' Matthew took out his cigarette case, then apparently changed his mind and slipped it back into his pocket as he glanced at her with narrowed eyes. 'I trust my own judgment.'

Tessa lowered her lashes to hide the tears which had sprung unbidden to her eyes. 'Thank you, Matthew.'

'That's the first time you've called me by my name,' he remarked quietly.

'I'm sorry.'

'Don't be.' She detected a note in his voice that puzzled her. 'I have no objections.'

The silence was somehow charged as it lengthened between them, and Tessa shifted uncomfortably from one foot to the other. 'May I go now?'

'Yes . . . and, Tessa . . .' He hesitated, coming towards her and, to her surprise, he framed her face gently with his hands. 'Now that I've heard you play the piano, I shall expect you to play more often.' Tessa held her breath as she looked up into his eyes, wondering what lay behind that unfathomable expression. Matthew Craig was a strange man of many moods, she thought. Would she ever understand him?

He dropped his hands to his sides and stepped away from her, his expression shuttered. 'Goodnight.'

Tessa whispered 'Goodnight' and escaped to her room as quickly as possible. The night was still and scented, and remarkably warm for June when the rest of the country was shivering in the winter cold. She sighed and undressed swiftly. It had been wonderful to play the piano again; to find the relief she so desperately needed. If Matthew had not arrived at that moment, she might have played on for hours, savouring the pure delight of being able to speak her emotions in that way.

Would Matthew keep his promise and not question her further? she wondered. 'Oh, yes, he will,' her heart cried with certainty. The most unfortunate part was that she had had to confess that she was not a housekeeper by profession, but her true identity still remained a secret, which was something to be thankful for. She could still be accepted as an ordinary girl, and perhaps be ... loved for herself?

Tessa literally shook herself. What on earth was she thinking of? She was not searching for love in particular, and if she was, then from whom? Matthew? 'Certainly not!' she told herself sternly, yet she had a disturbing vision of green eyes sparkling with humour, glittering with anger, or merely gazing at her with that unfathomable expression while they endeavoured to search his very soul.

'Oh, damn Matthew Craig for being so disturbingly

attractive,' she whispered to herself angrily. She was still emotionally unprepared for entanglements of that nature.

A frightening thought took possession of her. Matthew was attractive, confident, dependable, and the epitome of masculinity and, in her confused, emotional state, he was systematically breaking down the superficial barriers she had erected as protection against the world. She would have to be more careful in future, she decided. Especially where Matthew was concerned.

Barry strolled into the kitchen at the first light of dawn the following morning and combed his fingers through his tousled brown hair. 'Any hope of getting breakfast at this hour?' he grinned boyishly, pulling out a chair and seating himself at the table.

'This is unusually early for you,' Tessa remarked casually, breaking two eggs into the pan and pushing it on to the fire. 'What time did you get home last night?'

'Just before midnight, I think.' He stifled a yawn and helped himself to a slice of toast while he waited for Tessa to dish up the eggs.

'How was the chess last night?'

'I won, naturally,' Barry replied, pushing out his chest in a mock display of superiority. 'I'm unbeatable.'

'And conceited,' she laughed affectionately, handing him his breakfast.

'You've mortally wounded my pride,' he moaned, slapping a hand over his heart. 'I thought you liked me?'

84

'I do like you,' she replied with mock solemnity. 'Even though you're conceited.'

'I like you too,' he retaliated, 'even though you're cheeky.'

Their companionable laughter filled the kitchen briefly as Tessa helped herself to her own breakfast.

'Has Napoleon had breakfast yet?' Barry asked eventually, helping himself to another cup of coffee.

'Napoleon?' Tessa's glance was bewildered.

'Yes, Napoleon, the emperor of the estate,' Barry explained dramatically. 'Otherwise known as Matthew.'

'You shouldn't speak of your brother like that!' Tessa reprimanded sharply. Barry's meaningless and rather senseless remark had somehow shocked and hurt her, as though it had been directed at her personally.

'Oh, ho!' his eyes widened mischievously. 'Don't tell me you've developed a soft spot for big brother Matthew?'

The blood rushed painfully to her cheeks. 'Don't be silly!'

'Am I being silly?' he persisted laughingly.

'Your brother works very hard,' Tessa argued, endeavouring to change the subject, 'and never once has he passed such a disparaging remark about you.'

'My, my, my,' he shook his head, his eyes mirroring amusement. 'You *are* on your high horse, aren't you? I never realised old Matthew had such a strong ally in you.'

Tessa expelled the air from her lungs. 'I'm sorry, Barry, I didn't mean to snap at you. I was merely surprised and shocked by what you called him.'

She stared at him rather helplessly, unable to convey

the true reason for her reaction to his remark, for she could explain it even less to herself. What on earth had possessed her to react in that way? she asked herself admonishingly.

'Don't let it bother you, Tessa,' Barry said, winking and patting her shoulder comfortingly. 'I understand.'

Long after Barry had left Tessa still remained standing where she was, staring frowningly down at the table. What was it that Barry understood? What had her reaction conveyed to him, while it certainly succeeded in eluding her? Did he perhaps imagine that she was in love with Matthew? What an absolutely ridiculous thought! Matthew Craig meant nothing to her! Nothing at all!

CHAPTER FIVE

WHILE having tea on the patio one afternoon, Mrs Craig remarked casually, 'You haven't played the piano again since the other evening. You played so beautifully that I hoped you would play more often.'

'I don't want to make a nuisance of myself,' Tessa replied bashfully, wondering whether Matthew had told her of their discussion afterwards.

'Good heavens, Tessa, I did say you could play whenever you wished.'

'Yes, I know.' Her heart warmed towards her employer. 'You're very kind.'

'I'm not being kind at all, but entirely selfish. I was thinking particularly of my own enjoyment.' Ethel Craig glanced at her speculatively. 'You play exceptionally well. Have you ever given a recital before?'

Tessa's brain raced frantically in search of a suitable reply. 'I ... have thought of opening a school of music.'

'And you've very cleverly avoided answering my question,' her employer smiled resignedly.

Tessa averted her glance, her hands hovering over the tea pot. 'Would you care for another cup of tea?'

Ethel Craig nodded. 'Yes, please, my dear, and ... oh, that must be Matthew. He said he wouldn't be in town too long.'

The sound of a car could be heard approaching the house and Tessa automatically set out another cup. The Mercedes came up the drive and she noticed at once the blonde head of a girl in the passenger seat beside Matthew.

'He's not alone,' she murmured, almost to herself, her hands stilled over the tea things.

'Oh, how lovely!' Mrs Craig exclaimed joyously. 'He's brought Angela with him.'

Tessa stared with sincere admiration at the girl walking towards them with her arm linked through Matthew's. Her youthful figure was clad in a crimson dress that displayed every curve to perfection, and which was obviously not bought off the peg as was the sensible linen frock Tessa was wearing at that moment. Grey eyes, with a touch of haughtiness in them, looked beyond Tessa towards Mrs Craig, and crimson lips parted to display flashing white teeth.

So this was Angela Sinclair, Tessa thought, spellbound. It was no wonder that Matthew was interested, for she was remarkably beautiful. Matthew's glance met Tessa's only briefly before returning to the girl beside him, and to Tessa that innocent gesture meant complete exclusion. Something twisted sharply and inexplicably within her breast and she lowered her head quickly.

'Hello there, Mrs Craig,' Angela's melodious voice greeted as they stepped on to the patio. 'I hope you don't mind, but I've been invited to dinner.'

'My dear, you're always welcome, you know that,' Mrs Craig replied warmly, introducing Tessa.

The introduction was acknowledged by a brief nod of Angela's blonde head while her keen glance swiftly summed up the enemy as a possible opponent. 'I never thought that in this day and age one could still acquire such a thing as a housekeeper-companion?'.

'It was necessary, with Mother incapacitated as she is at the moment,' Matthew cut in briskly, pulling out a chair for her.

Angela subsided gracefully into the cushions of the cane chair and crossed her shapely legs, taking no further notice of Tessa, whose lowly position, in her eyes, warranted no further attention.

'I'll make a fresh pot of tea,' Tessa murmured hastily, and escaped to the kitchen, leaving the three of them chatting amicably on the patio.

Angela Sinclair had certainly managed to put her firmly in her place, Tessa thought wryly as she pushed the kettle on to the fire and rinsed the teapot. 'This is what you wanted, isn't it?' she asked herself sternly. 'Didn't you want to escape from the insincere smiles and polite chit-chat of recognition merely because you were Philip Ashton-Smythe's daughter?' Yes, she had wanted to escape. She had wanted to be herself, and to be accepted for herself. If Angela Sinclair looked upon her as nothing but a servant, then it was entirely a sincere reaction, and sincerity was far more acceptable to her at that moment.

Tessa sighed and filled the teapot once more, placing it on the tray along with a fresh jug of milk and an extra cup made of delicate china.

'Could I help you carry the tray?'

Tessa swung round sharply to find Matthew standing behind her, his tweed jacket accentuating the width of his shoulders, his grey slacks immaculately pressed and, as always, his expression unfathomable, if not slightly mocking.

'I get paid to carry trays about and to do various other chores in the house, remember?' Tessa reminded

89

him sharply, tilting her chin proudly.

There was no mistaking the mockery in Matthew's eyes as he appraised her. 'You don't like being put in your place, do you?' he guessed accurately and, illogically, this angered Tessa.

'I don't mind being put in my place, but I object most strongly to your offer of help,' she told him coldly. 'I know my place. Do you know yours?'

She could have willingly kicked herself at that moment for allowing her tongue to run away with her.

'You're treading on dangerous ground, Tessa,' he warned harshly, his face dark with anger as he seemingly towered above her menacingly. 'I shall not tolerate being spoken to like that, least of all from a subordinate like yourself.'

Tessa sucked her breath in sharply. She had deserved that reprimand, she realised, but it had none the less had the power to hurt her. Oh, why could she not have accepted his offer gracefully without passing all those disparaging remarks? Why had she allowed Angela's attitude to rattle her in this way?

'I'm sorry,' she murmured, biting her trembling lower lip. 'I had no right to speak to you like that, and I apologise.'

Matthew's green eyes regarded her with some speculation. 'What's the matter, Tessa? Why have you suddenly become so touchy?'

'I'm *not* touchy.'

'Oh, yes, you are,' he insisted as he swung her round to face him. 'And if I'm any good at reading the signs, I would say you took one look at Angela and went green with envy.'

'That's an absolutely absurd assumption!' Tessa

argued strongly, her pulse rate quickening rapidly at his closeness. 'There's really nothing about Angela Sinclair that I need to be envious about.'

He laughed softly and knowingly, and Tessa raised her eyes no higher than the tanned column of his throat. He released her suddenly and, before she realised what he was about to do, he had taken her face in his hands and kissed her lightly on the lips.

'I told you once before that, dressed in the right clothes, you could be more than attractive,' he laughed down into her startled face. 'Would it make you feel any better if I told you you had beautiful eyes?'

Tessa's heart hammered wildly against her ribs. 'You're deliberately making fun of me.'

'Perhaps just a little,' he admitted, releasing her and placing some distance between them.

'That's not very kind of you,' she remarked unevenly, her lips still tingling from his kiss, and her emotions riding roughshod over all sensible warning issued from her brain.

'You're a mystery, Tessa Smith,' he echoed the words Barry had uttered shortly after her arrival on the farm. 'Can you blame me if, at times, I'm suspicious of you, and also perhaps a little unkind?'

Tessa could not reply, but merely stared at him helplessly while she prayed frantically that he would not notice the effect he had upon her. Every nerve in her body seemed to vibrate with awareness, and an unaccustomed desire for ... understanding? No, it was something more than that. It was something she refused to analyse at that moment.

She sighed heavily and turned from him. 'The tea is getting cold, and your mother will wonder what's happened to us,' she remarked tonelessly.

'I'll take the tray,' Matthew said firmly, and this time she did not argue as he picked up the tray, motioning her to walk ahead of him.

'Oh, you've brought fresh tea at last,' Mrs Craig remarked instantly as they stepped on to the patio. 'What kept you so long?'

Tessa glanced swiftly in Matthew's direction as if challenging him to say something, but his face remained expressionless as he placed the tray on the table and seated himself beside Angela. Only now did his eyes meet hers and his glance was mocking as he waited expectantly for her to take up his mother's remark. He was enjoying her embarrassment, she realised, as a familiar anger seethed beneath the surface of her emotions. He had once again set a trap for her while he sat waiting patiently for her to step into it.

'The kettle took longer to boil than I'd anticipated,' Tessa mumbled nervously as Mrs Craig's curious glance persisted. 'I'm sorry you had to wait so long.'

Fortunately Mrs Craig appeared to be satisfied, but it was Angela Sinclair now who was regarding Tessa closely. Tessa's hand trembled as she poured the tea and she hated Matthew anew for keeping her so long in the kitchen and bringing about this awkward situation. Oh, how she hated him! But, at this point, it was Matthew who drew the attention away from her as he engaged Angela and his mother in conversation. She was confused by this sudden relenting on his part, and the tears swam in her eyes and she hastily excused herself to return to the kitchen.

She would never understand Matthew Craig, she

told herself as she reached the kitchen and dabbed at her eyes with her handkerchief. One minute he was out to trap her, and the next he offered protection. Her own feelings were even less understandable, for he could awaken the most violent hatred within her one moment, only to dash it away by one kind gesture. His anger frightened her, yet his smile had the power to spread a warm glow throughout her entire body. Never had anyone disturbed her in this way—not even Jeremy, whom she had once thought she loved. Their relationship had been warm, friendly and comfortable. Not once had her pulse rate quickened at his mere presence, not even the warmth of his kisses had succeeded in doing that, she realised for the first time, and the knowledge came as quite a shock. Their relationship had been entirely without passion—without love!

Tessa covered her burning cheeks with trembling hands. She *had* loved Jeremy, she insisted to herself, but not in the way she ... No! she groaned, cringing inwardly at the devastating realisation sweeping through her. Oh, no, she could not be in love with Matthew! It was impossible! He had done absolutely nothing to encourage this feeling, and yet she had been aware of his overpowering magnetism from the first moment she had looked into his peculiar green eyes. But why, oh, why? Why did it have to be Matthew?

Her temples were throbbing painfully as she continued preparing the evening meal. It felt as though someone had struck her a violent blow that left her weak and trembling, and filled her with the uncontrollable desire to escape before it was too late.

Daisy entered the kitchen at that crucial moment,

her green overall spotlessly clean, her white apron starched and crackling with every movement she made. Tessa had never been more thankful to see her black face than at that moment. Where her hands fumbled, Daisy took over with competence, and somehow between them they managed to prepare the dinner, for Tessa was unable to concentrate on the task before her while her thoughts leapt continuously to Matthew. His image came between her and the cooking pots, and no matter how much she tried, she could not erase the sight of his fair hair brushed back severely from his forehead, the strong line of his jaw, and the way his green eyes crinkled at the corners when he smiled.

'Missie! Missie!' Daisy finally managed to penetrate her thoughts. 'The potatoes are burning!'

Tessa snatched up a cloth and removed the pot from the stove in the nick of time. She really would have to concentrate on what she was doing, she told herself firmly, or Angela Sinclair might have to be satisfied with burnt offerings. She giggled suddenly with unexpected lightheartedness which seemed to perplex Daisy even further.

Having dinner with the Craigs and their lovely guest that evening was an agonising experience for Tessa. The discovery that she loved Matthew increased her awareness of him, and it was with the greatest difficulty that she managed not to glance in his direction too often. The apparent ease with which he and Angela communicated sent little stabs of jealousy through her. It was an emotion she had never experienced before and it merely added to her discomfort.

Barry, seated beside Angela, seemed rather reticent and, with the conversation flowing steadily, no one appeared to notice that neither Barry nor Tessa was contributing towards it. Except for glaring occasionally in Angela's direction, Barry practically ignored her, and Tessa, over-sensitive to the atmosphere, wondered if he, too, was not in love with Angela Sinclair. She was certainly attractive and, with her sparkling personality, she held Matthew's attention, as well as Mrs Craig's, with seemingly no effort at all.

On several occasions Tessa found Angela regarding her steadily and, for some reason, her close scrutiny had the power to shake Tessa's composure to such an extent that her hands trembled visibly, causing her to drop her knife on one occasion which afforded her a curiously mocking glance from Matthew that sent the blood rushing to her cheeks.

Tessa brought in the coffee and met again Angela's disturbingly curious glance. A little shiver of warning went through her which she tried valiantly to ignore.

'The dinner was excellent, Tessa,' Mrs Craig complimented her while they drank their coffee. 'I really don't know what I shall do once I'm able to take over the housekeeping again. I can just imagine all the complaints!'

'Mrs Craig, you flatter me,' Tessa laughed nervously. 'I'm sure you're merely being modest, and that you're really an excellent cook yourself.'

'To be an excellent cook one must love it.' Mrs Craig pulled a face. 'I've always hated it.'

There were exclamations of disbelief from the others and a certain amount of teasing until Matthew remarked quite casually, 'If you dislike cooking so intensely, Mother, why don't you offer Tessa a permanent job?'

There was a brief, shocked silence while everyone considered his suggestion. To Tessa it felt as though a trap had been sprung and she held her breath, waiting for the final clinch which would offer no escape.

'What do you think of that suggestion, Tessa?' Mrs Craig asked calmly when the silence began to lengthen unbearably. 'Would you consider remaining permanently?'

Tessa was once again at the centre of attention and she clenched her hands beneath the table until the nails bit into her palms. 'I ... well, I—' she swallowed with difficulty. 'I'm afraid I—can't remain here longer than the six weeks originally agreed to.'

'Why not?' Matthew demanded quietly. 'Have you another job waiting for you when you leave here?'

'No, I ... I haven't.'

Matthew's expression became incredulous. 'Let's get this straight. You say you can't remain here longer than you were actually required, yet you have no other job waiting for you.' He leaned slightly towards Tessa and she could feel his glance scorching her. 'Could you perhaps be a little more explicit?'

She was all at once floundering in deep waters, and for the moment she had no idea how she would be able to save herself. Across the table Barry's glance was sympathetic—bless him! Mrs Craig looked on expectantly, while Angela displayed a certain amount of boredom, and Matthew waited with tight-lipped determination.

As if from a distance, Tessa heard herself say, 'I would like to find employment a little closer to home.'

'That's understandable, my dear,' Mrs Craig accepted her explanation readily, but Matthew adopted a rather sceptical attitude.

'Miss Smith.' It was the first time Angela had actually spoken to her directly and Tessa felt her nerves tightening like a coil at the other girl's pensive stare. 'Forgive me, but haven't we met somewhere before?'

'I don't think so,' Tessa managed calmly, hiding the turmoil within her.

'Your face is terribly familiar,' Angela continued unperturbed. 'Especially now that I've had the opportunity to observe you closely.'

Tessa shot an apprehensive glance in Matthew's direction. Angela's casual remark had awakened his own suspicions and would invariably act as encouragement for him to pursue his quest to discover the truth.

'Miss Sinclair,' Tessa replied smoothly, directing her steady glance at the other girl, 'I have an excellent memory for faces, and I'm positive that I've never seen you before in my life.'

'You must have a double, Tessa,' Barry laughed away the awkward silence that followed.

'It seems so,' Tessa smiled at him thankfully. 'More coffee, anyone?'

Tessa remained in the kitchen that evening until Daisy had left for home, then she, too, slipped out through the back door and went for a quiet walk in the garden. The air was cool, fresh, and mysteriously soothing as she strolled through the garden with its rolling lawns and near tropical shrubs. What blessed peace it was to be part of this enveloping, mitigating silence after the emotionally disturbing hour at dinner. It was becoming exceedingly difficult to continue with this life of pretence. Because of their persistent questioning she had had to wrap herself in a cocoon of mystery which she was beginning to hate, for she was essentially an honest person. Her father had been right after all, it could lead to disastrous difficulties if one ventured out on an expedition of deceit, however innocent.

'It seems as though I'm not the only one in need of fresh air,' Barry's voice interrupted her thoughts as he loomed up beside her in the darkness.

'I thought I'd take a quick stroll through the garden before your mother needs me,' Tessa told him guiltily.

'Aren't you going to join us in the living-room until then?' he asked, falling into step beside her.

'You have a guest this evening,' Tessa reminded him. 'Besides, it's not really my place.'

Barry caught hold of her arm and pulled her round to face him. 'What do you mean, it's not your place?' he demanded, frowning down at her in the moonlight.

Tessa shrugged her shoulders beneath the silky blouse. 'I'm an employee in your mother's home ... a servant.'

'Don't be silly!' he exclaimed vehemently. 'You're more than a servant in our home. You've been like one of the family.'

Tessa blinked at the tears that sprang to her eyes. 'Thank you, Barry,' she whispered jerkily. 'That's one of the nicest things anyone has said to me for a long time.'

'I mean it, Tessa,' he insisted seriously. 'You *are* one of the family.'

'I don't somehow think Matthew will agree with you,' she laughed shakily, trying to imagine Matthew making that sweeping statement, and failing.

'Who cares what Matthew thinks?' Barry remarked dismissively.

'I do,' the words sprang to Tessa's lips, but she bit them back swiftly. 'Angela is very lovely, isn't she?' she remarked instead, bringing the conversation on to safer ground as they continued their walk.

Barry appeared to stiffen beside her. 'Yes.'

'Matthew must love her very much,' Tessa tried again, realising that she was openly fishing to find out more about their lengthy relationship.

The silence lengthened ominously between them and Tessa was beginning to wonder if she had not overstepped the mark somewhat by delving too deeply into their personal life.

'Matthew doesn't love Angela,' Barry said eventually, and Tessa could not prevent the little thrill of hope that quivered through her.

'What makes you say that?'

Barry lit a cigarette and smoked silently for a while. 'If Matthew loved her, he would have married her long ago,' he argued. 'Instead he's kept her dangling on a string for more than two years.'

'Perhaps she's not ready to settle down,' Tessa suggested tentatively.

'Oh, she's ready to settle down, all right,' Barry laughed briefly, 'but with the right man.'

'Oh?' Tessa was at a loss to understand the implication of his brash statement.

Barry drew hard on his cigarette. 'I might as well tell you that I intend marrying her.' Tessa drew her breath in sharply as he continued, 'Matthew has had more than enough time to make up his mind about her, now it's my turn. We are, after all, more suited to each other.'

Tessa detected a note of arrogance in his voice as she expelled her breath slowly. 'You seem very sure of yourself. How do you know she'll reciprocate your feelings, and that you won't merely succeed in driving her further into Matthew's arms?'

'Where do you think I've been spending all these evenings I've been out?' Barry laughed with self-assurance as they approached the house.

'With—with Angela?' Tessa guessed hesitantly, her mind reeling.

Barry stopped in his stride and smiled down at her. 'Right first time.'

'But—but I thought—the other evening when you went out to play chess——' Tessa floundered to a halt.

'Oh, that was the truth,' Barry admitted, 'but not the other evenings.'

'Oh.' What else was there to say? Despite the gentle fluttering of hope in her breast, there was a feeling of intense pity in her heart for Matthew. What if he actually *did* love Angela? Would he take kindly to losing her to Barry?

'Not a word of this to anyone, do you hear?' Barry warned, flinging his cigarette to the ground and crushing it beneath the heel of his shoe.

'But why the secrecy?'

'Well ...' he hesitated a moment, kicking at a stone to hide his embarrassment. 'If Matthew does happen to love Angela, we wouldn't like to spring this on him suddenly. It would perhaps be kinder and easier to accept if it all happened gradually.'

'Is that why you practically ignored each other this evening?' Tessa asked, beginning to understand, and with a feeling of warmth towards Barry for his unexpected consideration concerning Matthew's feelings.

'That's right.' Barry tugged at a curl beside her ear. 'By the way,' he smiled mischievously, 'temperamentally, you and Matthew are ideally suited.'

Tessa gasped at the audacity of his statement, but Barry gave her no time to reply, for he turned immediately and went indoors. For a time she lingered outside, trying to still the violent beating of her heart and at the same time forcing herself not to dwell on his teasing remark. On reaching the kitchen she thought again of Barry's confession that he and Angela loved each other. If it were true that Matthew did not care for Angela, would she, Tessa, stand a chance? Her cheeks went hot at the thought. Matthew was beyond her reach, and the sooner she realised this the better. He was suspicious of her and continually tried to trap her into a confession, why then would he lower himself to care for his mother's housekeeper?

Oh, it was all so silly, so futile, her heart cried. She wanted to be loved for herself, yet now the very fact that she was acting a part in search of her objective was counting against her.

The low murmur of their voices reached her in the

101

kitchen where she stood about restlessly until Mrs Craig should send for her. What were they talking about? she wondered, filling the kettle in case more tea would be required. No matter how much she tried she could not banish Matthew from her thoughts, and the discovery of her love for him merely sharpened her senses and drove all sensible thoughts from her mind.

The sound of footsteps came down the passage towards the kitchen and every nerve in her body told her that it was Matthew. When he entered the kitchen moments later it was no surprise to her, and she could merely stand there staring at him as if she were seeing him for the first time.

'I thought that you would join us in the living-room after dinner,' he began, that familiar glint of mockery in his eyes. 'Angela was most anxious to hear you play the piano when we told her of your expertise.'

'My apologies for having to disappoint Miss Sinclair,' Tessa replied with a touch of sarcasm in her voice, her only weapon against his mockery.

Matthew's glance was thoughtful, his eyes slightly narrowed. 'What has Angela done that you should dislike her in this way?'

Tessa drew her breath in sharply. 'I don't dislike An—I mean Miss Sinclair.'

'Angela will do,' he snapped impatiently. 'No one stands on ceremony hereabouts.' He leaned against the table and folded his arms. 'Angela can swear that she has seen you somewhere before, and I have asked her to pursue that line of thought.'

Tessa's heart leapt to her throat, and her voice, when it came, was a broken whisper. 'Why?'

Matthew shrugged his broad shoulders. 'Call it curiosity, if you like.'

Quite innocently, Angela had become a threat to Tessa's happiness, a happiness so fragile that it could crumble beneath the slightest hint of deceit. A cold hand gripped her heart as the silence lengthened between them and, for the first time, Tessa noticed an expression other than mockery in Matthew's eyes. It was an expression that sent her heart galloping wildly and suffused her cheeks with colour. She lowered her lashes swiftly. Whatever happens, Matthew must not be allowed to see what lay in her heart, for his mockery of her love would hurt more deeply than anything had ever done before, or ever would in the future.

'Haven't I proved myself capable of looking after your mother and your home?' she asked pleadingly, a slight tremor in her voice as she fixed her glance on the top button of his shirt.

Matthew was silent for several seconds before replying. 'You've proved yourself in your capacity as housekeeper-companion, but not as a person.'

'I see.' Her breath came unevenly over parted lips. 'You still doubt me, then?'

She had no doubt that Angela Sinclair would eventually discover her true identity. She had been insistent enough at dinner about having seen Tessa somewhere prior to her arrival at the Craig residence, and she would pursue this thought relentlessly, and with Matthew's encouragement. But, until then, Tessa was forced to continue with the charade. To tell the truth now would mean that she would have to leave and, quite probably, never see Matthew again, and for this reason she wanted to delay her departure as much as possible.

Matthew unfolded his arms and moved away from the table. 'I don't doubt you, I just wish I knew more about you.' Again that brief, uncomfortable silence. 'I actually came to tell you that I'm taking Angela home, and that Mother is ready for bed.'

'Oh, I'll come at once.' She made a dash for the door, but Matthew stopped her.

'You'd better remove the kettle from the stove unless you want it to boil dry,' he reminded her mockingly.

'Oh, yes.' She was in such a hurry to get away from him that she blushed furiously at her forgetfulness. 'I —I thought you might all want something more to drink,' she explained hastily while removing the kettle from the fire.

'Not at the moment,' he assured her evenly, 'but I wouldn't mind a cup of coffee when I get back from town.'

Did he expect her to wait up for him, or was he merely teasing? she wondered breathlessly as she hovered on the verge of escape, but Matthew answered this question almost as if he had read her thoughts.

'You can leave the kettle to one side of the stove and I'll make my own coffee before going to bed, so there's no reason for you to wait up for me.'

Tessa swallowed nervously and escaped as quickly as she could, not waiting to see whether Matthew was following her. Before entering the living-room, she stopped for a moment to pass a trembling hand over her hot face. It would not do to confront Mrs Craig before she had complete control over her wayward emotions.

CHAPTER SIX

DURING the third week in July Mrs Craig had the plaster cast removed from her leg, but the strain of having to become accustomed to walking again made her doctor insist that Tessa should remain with her for at least another two weeks. Tessa was secretly overjoyed by this decision although she was careful not to display her feelings in Matthew's presence.

It was during that same week that Barry would be celebrating his birthday, and what better way was there to celebrate it than by inviting a few of his friends and having a barbecue, Barry had suggested. Matthew was opposed to this idea at first, but when Tessa offered to help with the preparations, he eventually relented.

'I don't want Mother to become involved in this caper and overtaxing her strength in the process,' he warned Tessa when he found her alone in the kitchen.

'I shan't let her do a thing,' Tessa promised him, her lips curving into a smile as she noticed the disagreeable frown creasing his brow. 'You look like the proverbial bear with a sore head,' she laughed up at him. 'Surely you don't object to Barry having a few friends over on his birthday?'

'Naturally I don't,' he gestured angrily. 'I was merely thinking of the extra work.'

'Why don't you let me worry about that?' she teased gently, a glimmer of laughter in her eyes. 'Preparing food for hungry people, no matter what the occasion, is what I get paid for, isn't it?'

Her shoulders were suddenly gripped so tightly that she almost cried out in pain. 'If you ever pass a remark like that again, I'll——'

'Yes?' she challenged, a pulse throbbing wildly in her throat at the exquisite agony of his touch. 'You'll what?'

For interminable second angry green eyes met questioning blue ones and then, unexpectedly, Tessa found herself clasped hard against his hard chest. Before she could cry out he had lowered his fair head and those stern lips claimed hers in a bruising kiss that seared through her very soul. His kiss was a punishment that left no room for tenderness, and Tessa felt the hopeless tears burning behind her closed eyelids.

He released her as suddenly as he had taken her and Tessa, swaying slightly, stared up at him through a film of tears.

'I've never been able to resist a challenge,' Matthew said thickly, his chest heaving slightly. 'So be warned!'

He turned on his heel and left the kitchen while Tessa raised gentle fingers to her bruised lips before dashing away the trace of her tears with the back of her hand. For several minutes she stood there motionless, unable to think, until the most awe-inspiring thought took possession of her. If Matthew could create such havoc to her emotions with a kiss of punishment, then what would happen if he should kiss her as though he really wanted to? It was a tantalising thought that set her nerves tingling and brought a quivering smile to her lips.

Barry walked into the kitchen moments later. 'I've drawn up a list of people I would like to invite, and——' He stopped short and peered at Tessa speculatively where she stood in the middle of the floor staring into space. 'If I weren't so sure that there was no one else about other than myself and dry-as-dust Matthew, I would hazard a guess and say that you were in love.'

Tessa surfaced with difficulty and stared at him foolishly, the colour mounting in her cheeks as Barry subjected her to an even closer scrutiny. She saw the laughter leave his eyes to be replaced by astonishment.

'Oh, no!' he groaned, peering down at her. 'Don't tell me you have fallen for Matthew?'

It was a statement rather than a question and Tessa, for once, was at a loss for words, realising that her silence could only indicate that his supposition was correct.

'Tessa, Tessa,' Barry shook his head at her, the teasing glint returning to his grey eyes. 'If you'd fallen in love with me, I would have understood that it was my sparkling personality that did the trick ... but Matthew? He's always so serious and gloomy, without the slightest idea how to relax and enjoy himself!'

'Perhaps he's never been given the opportunity to do so,' Tessa proffered in Matthew's defence, her chin lifting determinedly.

Barry smiled an infuriating, knowing smile, and did not pursue the subject. 'Here's that list I mentioned,' he said instead, dropping a sheet of paper on the scrubbed table. 'You'll see that I've invited only four couples, as well as Angela.'

'You mentioned a barbecue,' Tessa prompted, gathering her wits about her.

'Yes, but that part of it you can leave to me,' he smiled mischievously. 'I'll get the meat, light the fire, and play open air chef for that night. I shall be the perfect host, and I shall live up to brother Matthew's expectations in every way.'

'Oh, Barry,' Tessa moaned, 'I wish you'd be serious.'

'But I am!' he insisted adamantly. 'All you'll have to do is make the salads and supply the eats for later in the evening. How's that?'

'Sounds fine to me,' she laughed. 'And what about a birthday cake?'

'Oh, really, Tessa!' his eyes rolled towards the ceiling. 'At my age? A cake with twenty-five candles on it?'

'What's wrong with that?' Tessa demanded. 'At my mother's last birthday party she had a cake with forty-six candles on it, and none of the guests thought it strange.'

'Oh, really?'

His glance was expectant as if he were waiting for her to divulge further information, but Tessa closed up instantly. 'Take your list,' she said briskly, 'and start telephoning your friends while I plan the salads.'

'Don't take too long with the planning,' he winked at her. 'D-Day is the day after tomorrow.'

'Don't I know it!' she sighed, literally pushing him out of the kitchen and setting to work.

Barry was on his best behaviour on the day of his birthday and Tessa was certain that Matthew would not find anything to complain about. She spent most of the day in the kitchen preparing the salads and savouries for

108

the barbecue, until it was time to assist Mrs Craig with her dressing. Tessa was hot and tired from the hours of standing on her feet in an overheated kitchen, and added to this her nose was shining and her face was flushed. From Mrs Craig's bedroom window she could see Barry packing the firewood in the barbecue on the front lawn, and Matthew, whom she had studiously avoided since their last encounter in the kitchen, had already left to collect Angela.

Except for Barry's carefree whistling, the house was suddenly very quiet as Tessa hurried to her room to bath and change. A barbecue was normally a very casual affair, so Tessa selected a cream dress she had not worn before. The fabric was warm and silky and, unlike her other dresses, clung snugly to her slender waist. The neckline was modestly low while the sleeves widened at the wrists to be gathered tightly into a neat cuff.

She brushed her dark hair vigorously until it shone and took more than the usual care with her make-up, wrinkling her nose at the irrational thought that her efforts were for Matthew's benefit. 'Be a devil and behave a little less reserved towards Matthew this evening,' an impudent little voice urged. 'So what if he thinks your behaviour strange, you're leaving soon anyway,' the voice persisted. Tessa sobered instantly. This was the truth. She *would* be leaving soon ... within two weeks! Would it matter then what he thought of her, or if Angela had perhaps succeeded in discovering her true identity? After a moment of thought Tessa decided that, come what may, this was going to be her night as well as Barry's.

Matthew finally arrived with Angela, who was dressed

in an attractive blue slack suit which would no doubt draw the attention of the male guests. Her fair hair was beautifully combed and piled on top of her head, leaving only a single coil hanging down her back. Shortly afterwards Barry's other guests arrived. There were three young married couples from Idwala, and the fourth couple was a young farmer from the district with his girl-friend.

It was a delightfully warm evening for this open-air occasion and Tessa had placed chairs on the lawn, just off the patio. Barry started the fire and then, like the perfect host he intended being that evening, he offered his guests something to drink. Tessa settled Mrs Craig comfortably in a chair beside Angela and then went through to the kitchen for a last-minute check that everything was in order.

Barry was pouring the drinks in the living-room when Tessa returned and, as he had been doing all day, he was whistling to himself.

'Angela looks stunningly beautiful this evening,' she remarked as she was about to pass him.

'Yes, she does,' Barry agreed enthusiastically, turning to face her. 'Hey! You're not so bad yourself when you doll yourself up,' he smiled, taking in her appearance. 'Is this for Matthew's benefit?'

'Don't be silly!' Her cheeks reddened.

'I'll tell you something,' Barry continued seriously. 'I saw him staring at you just now and I could almost hear the ice melting around his heart.'

Tessa placed her hands against her flaming cheeks. 'Stop it, Barry!'

'It's the truth,' he insisted in earnest. 'With a little

bit of encouragement you'll have him eating out of your tiny little hand.'

Tessa's heart was thudding heavily against her ribs as she followed Barry outside. Matthew was standing beside his mother's chair listening attentively to something Angela was saying, and Tessa was certain that Barry had merely been teasing.

Everyone appeared to be in a party mood and there was much laughter from the men as they stood about the fire. The women were not to be left out as they drew their chairs closer to Ethel Craig's and giggled incessantly at Angela's sharp sense of humour.

'Hey, Tessa!' Barry called. 'Be a chum and bring the meat, the fire's ready.'

'I'll help you, Tessa,' Angela surprisingly offered as she followed Tessa indoors.

'I will take the meat if you will take the salads out on to the patio,' Tessa suggested thankfully. 'You can place them on the tables I've put there for this purpose.'

Angela had lost her apparent haughtiness of their first meeting and Tessa found herself liking her more as the evening progressed. The delectable aroma of meat grilling on an open fire permeated the air and everyone sniffed appreciatively.

'My parents love having a barbecue,' Angela remarked pleasantly to Tessa as they sat watching Barry turning the meat. 'Meat is so expensive these days, though, that it's becoming almost a luxury. I suppose it's even more expensive in Johannesburg?'

'At times, yes, I suppose so.' Tessa felt trapped. She could not be more definite, for she had never had any need to bother about the culinary purchases for the house. Her mother always saw to the household accounts and Tessa had never thought to question her about the prices.

'I believe you'll be leaving us soon,' Angela continued, sipping lightly at her drink. 'Mrs Craig will miss you, I'm certain of that.'

Mrs Craig may miss her, yes, Tessa thought sadly. Only Mrs Craig? Would Matthew miss her too, or would it make no difference to him whether she was there or not? She caught sight of his imposing figure towering out above the others beside the fire, and her heart twisted savagely.

'Will you be going to a similar type of job?'

'Perhaps,' Tessa replied vaguely, and was fortunately saved from further questioning by Barry announcing that the meat was done.

Tessa remained close to Mrs Craig for the rest of the evening where she sat just within the circle of guests. They laughed at Barry's clowning as he blew out his candles and then, like most parties, the carpet in the living-room was finally rolled up and the dancing began.

Matthew made his mother comfortable in the living-room where she would be able to watch the proceedings without being trampled, while Tessa brought out the savouries for those who wanted to nibble in between dances. For a time Barry manned the record player, but very soon he found a replacement and was dancing every dance with Angela. Tessa ventured a glance in Matthew's direction where he sat quietly smoking a cigarette, but he seemed quite unperturbed by the fact that the woman he loved had been annexed by his brother. Did he really not care, Tessa wondered

112

curiously, or was he merely putting up a brave front to hide his true feelings?

Ethel Craig's eyes sparkled as she watched the dancing. 'Do you know, Tessa,' she said eventually with a dreamy expression in her eyes, 'when I was young, my husband and I often had parties here and we used to dance right through the night until the following morning.'

'This was in the old house, I presume?'

'Yes.' Memories clouded her eyes. 'I must show you a photograph of the old house one day. It was built in the old colonial style and very fashionable in those days.'

'I sometimes get the feeling, Mother, that you much preferred the old house to this one,' Matthew remarked lazily from the recess of his armchair.

'Oh, but I didn't say that,' Ethel contradicted him hastily. 'I have nothing against modern houses, it's just that the old house held many memories for me, which this one doesn't.'

Matthew stretched his long legs out before him and looked exceedingly handsome in his dark blue shirt and grey slacks. 'Given time, this house will gather as many memories as the first one.'

'That will only begin to happen when the sound of children's voices echoes within these walls,' Mrs Craig remarked knowingly. 'I'm not getting any younger and I would still like to enjoy the company of my grand-children.'

Tessa experienced a peculiar sensation at the pit of her stomach that swept upwards to clutch agonisingly at her heart. The thought of Matthew married to someone else, someone who would bear his children, was un-

113

bearably painful, and totally unthinkable. She raised her glance suddenly to discover Matthew regarding her with a breath-stopping intensity that made her glance down nervously at her hands clenched so tightly in her lap.

'Perhaps, Mother, you won't have long to wait,' Matthew remarked evenly, and Tessa closed her eyes tightly as if to ward off the pain.

'I'll put the kettle on and make us something to drink,' she murmured after a moment, and escaped to the kitchen.

She filled the kettle mechanically, shutting her mind to the sound of the music and gaiety coming from the living-room, and to the disturbing thoughts crowding in on her. It would be better not to think, or feel, and merely to shut her heart and mind to all futile emotions.

She placed the kettle on the stove and at that moment an arm reached over her shoulder and moved it aside again. Firm hands, strong and determined, turned her about, and she found herself looking up into Matthew's green eyes, conveying something she could not define at that moment while her heart thudded uncomfortably against her ribs.

'It's too early to make tea,' he said. 'Would you do me the honour?'

How proper, how old-worldly, and how delightful the thought of being held in his arms, if for no other reason but to dance with him. 'I shall be honoured to dance with you,' she replied tremulously, a hint of humour nestling in her eyes.

Ethel Craig smiled her approval as Matthew's arm slipped about Tessa's waist, and then Tessa saw and heard no more except the slow rhythm of the music and the feel of Matthew's arm about her. Added to this was the devastating effect his nearness had on her pulse rate. Matthew did not dance with the flourish of some dancers she had known, but their steps matched well and Tessa, as his arms closed more firmly about her, relaxed against him and allowed herself to be swept along on a cloud of happiness. What did it matter that her happiness was to be brief, and who could blame her if, for these few minutes, she took with both hands whatever happiness should come her way? It would have to last her for ever, wouldn't it?

Strange, she thought dreamily, how the other dancers seemed to fade, leaving only the two of them on the floor. It was as though nothing, and no one existed beyond the shroud of this moment. Her pulse quickened. Did she imagine it, or had Matthew's lips brushed against her temple a moment ago? No, there it was again, the featherlight warmth of his lips brushing against her forehead. What did it mean? Was he, too, swept along by this moment in time, or was he perhaps imagining that the girl in his arms was Angela? Tessa drew away from him at this distasteful thought, her hand against his chest.

'What's wrong, Tessa?' he asked. 'Did I step on your toe?'

'N-no, it was nothing,' she stammered hopelessly. 'I was thinking of something.'

'Something unpleasant?'

'It was a silly thought, really,' she sighed, going back into his arms.

Without her realising it, he had steered her out on to

the patio into the moonlit darkness, and her heart fluttered suddenly like a frightened bird. The music stopped but instead of releasing her, he merely drew her closer to him. As the next record started her head went down on to his shoulder and it seemed inexplicably right that it should be there. Both his arms were about her now and she closed her eyes, inhaling the warm, male fragrance of him, and loving the feel of his muscular chest where she could detect the heavy beat of his heart beneath her fingertips.

They melted into the shadows of the bouganvillaea and stood still. For one heart stopping second Tessa waited and then Matthew lowered his head and his lips brushed against her own. It was a gentle, exploratory kiss that made her tremble with the sweetness of it, for it was quite unlike the harsh kiss he had bestowed upon her two days ago.

His mouth strayed across her cheek to her ear and then back again to claim her lips. This time his kiss was intensely passionate and deeply moving, awakening emotions within her she had not known existed. She was powerless to resist as his hands caressed her in a way no other man, not even Jeremy, had dared to do, and the knowledge both frightened and delighted her. Was this what loving was all about? She wondered ecstatically as she threaded her fingers through his hair. Was loving also this alarmingly wild desire to give, not only your love, but yourself ... wholeheartedly and completely?

Matthew released her then and Tessa's breath came unevenly over parted lips still warm and tingling from his kisses. Sanity returned painfully as she faced him in the darkness.

'Matthew, this is madness,' she breathed tremulously, turning away from him in an effort to shut off his irresistible magnetism.

'An irrefutably sweet madness,' he whispered, trailing his lips along the back of her neck and making her tremble.

'We must stop this,' she pleaded urgently even as she swayed back against him.

Matthew laughed softly into her neck as his hands closed about her waist. 'Why don't you admit that you are enjoying this as much as I am.'

Tessa tried to speak but could not force the words of denial past her unwilling lips. His hands moved upwards from her waist to where her breasts swelled gently against the silk of her dress, and Tessa was lost. She turned in his arms and gave him her lips with an urgency that surprised even herself. They kissed hungrily, demandingly, and Tessa's heart raced at such speed that she felt deliciously dizzy, wishing this moment would never end.

It was the sound of voices that finally made them draw apart. Dazed and bemused, she watched Barry and Angela, their arms about each other, strolling across the patio and into the shadowy garden. It was then that she became aware of Matthew's silent, statue-like frame beside her and a cold wave of reality swept over her. Barry and Angela could not have made their feelings for each other more obvious if they had tried, and in her heart Tessa wept for Matthew, as well as herself. It was then, too, that she realised how outrageously she had behaved by allowing Matthew to make love to her in the way he had. What must he be thinking of her? What he may have intended as a frustrated attempt at

117

a light flirtation, she had certainly made the most of, and in so doing she had made her feelings quite obvious. What on earth had possessed her? she wondered, squirming inwardly with intense humiliation.

'Perhaps we should go inside,' she suggested hollowly. 'We can't leave your mother unattended much longer.'

Mathew moved then, glancing down at her although his expression remained hidden from her in the shadows. 'Yes, let's go in,' he agreed briefly, walking a little distance away from her as if he could not bear to touch her even accidentally. Did he despise her that much? she wondered miserably.

Mrs Craig was showing signs of fatigue as they entered the living-room and Tessa went across to her with swift concern while Matthew poured himself a drink.

'If you don't mind, Tessa, I think I would like to go to bed,' she whispered apologetically.

'Of course, Mrs Craig,' Tessa agreed sympathetically. 'It has been a tiring and exciting day for you.'

Ethel Craig nodded and said 'goodnight' to Barry's guests before allowing Tessa to help her to her room.

'What has happened to Barry and Angela?' she asked Tessa when they were alone, and Tessa floundered momentarily before deciding on the truth.

'I think they went for a walk in the garden.'

Ethel Craig regarded her steadily for a moment before speaking. 'Do you think there is something between them? I have always thought that Matthew and Angela would some day——' She stopped and frowned heavily. 'I couldn't help noticing the way Barry and Angela behaved towards each other this evening, and when a man takes a pretty girl into the garden at night, it can mean only one thing. Am I right?'

'Yes, Mrs Craig, you are,' Tessa admitted quietly.

'Hm. I wonder what Matthew will say when he finds out?'

'I think Matthew knows already,' Tessa remarked wryly. 'We were on the patio when they came out, arms about each other and laughing happily as though they hadn't a care in the world.'

'Yes,' Mrs Craig said slowly, her eyes beginning to sparkle. 'I saw the two of you dance out on to the patio as well, *and* you remained out there for quite a long time.'

Tessa flushed deeply but refrained from commenting.

'Do you think this knowledge has hurt Matthew?' the older woman asked with concern.

Tessa hesitated a moment, recalling the change in his attitude when Barry and Angela came out on to the patio. 'Yes, I think it has. I think it has hurt him very much.'

'And what about your own hurt?' her selfish heart cried as she drew a swift, agonising breath before helping Mrs Craig to undress.

There was total disorder after everyone had left. Barry was on his way to Idwala with Angela, and Matthew sat slumped in a chair in the living-room, his brooding glance following Tessa's every movement as she cleared away the debris and restored the furniture to their rightful place. She was aware of his eyes following her about and it caused her considerable discomfort. In some way she would have to explain away her behaviour earlier that evening in an effort to restore their relationship to its previous footing. The problem was, how was she going to do that, and what could she say?

The simplest would be to say, 'Matthew, I love you, and that is the only reason I allowed you to make love to me. My apologies for confronting you with this unwanted and embarrassing confession, and forgive me if I now crawl into my little shell to die of shame.'

She could just imagine his reaction to a remark like that! His mockery would reign supreme, and she would be put in her place more smartly than ever before. What right had she, a servant, to nurture such feelings for him? What was he thinking as he sat there in that big armchair? she wondered distractedly. Was he thinking that his first impression of her character had been correct? With a little chill of horror she realised that she had made no effort to stave off his advances and had indeed welcomed his kisses. Her reactions could therefore only confirm his suspicions if he had planned their encounter as some sort of test. In the kitchen, away from his prying eyes, she considered this matter once more and could not bring herself to believe that he would stoop so low. No, she could not have misjudged him so completely.

Tessa glanced about her ruefully. There were dirty glasses, cups and plates all over the place. She glanced at her watch and sighed, it was almost midnight and, as much as she longed for her comfortable bed, she could not leave this mess for Daisy to clear up in the morning. She tied an apron about her waist, rolled up her sleeves, and set to work washing up the dirty dishes.

There was the sound of a step behind her and, to Tessa's surprise, Matthew picked up a towel and started drying. He was really the most incredible man she had ever met. She would never have imagined him the kind of man to do a menial job like drying dishes, and yet there was nothing odd about his helpful presence. He smiled briefly at the surprised glance she cast him and for the rest of the time they worked in silence. When everything was done, Tessa hoped that Matthew would leave, but he remained there, his presence making her agitated and nervy.

'Why doesn't he leave!' she wondered frantically as she restored everything to their proper places, but Matthew obviously had no intention of leaving as he leaned comfortably against the table and folded his arms across his chest. 'If only he would say something instead of following me about with those green eyes of his that never miss anything!'

How deeply had he been hurt by the knowledge that Angela preferred Barry? she wondered to herself. Had he perhaps suspected something, and was this the reason for his behaviour? She had to talk to him, she decided. She had to explain that she was not in the habit of allowing herself to get carried away emotionally as she had done earlier that evening.

Tessa undid her apron with trembling fingers and draped it over the back of a chair. 'Matthew, I would like to——' She turned as she spoke and found the light blotted out by his broad shoulders and, before she could prevent him, she found herself in his arms with his lips silencing her effectively. At first she was too startled to resist, then it took all her powers of concentration not to respond to lips that had already penetrated her defences so effectively.

Matthew raised his head a fraction to glance at her

questioningly and Tessa struggled free from his arms in that brief moment he had relaxed his hold.

'Matthew, I think——'

'Don't think, Tessa,' he interrupted, an unfathomable expression in his eyes as he breached the gap between them and placed his hands about her face. 'Let's throw all sensible arguments aside and make the most of this moment.'

Tessa stood immobile in his gentle clasp as he lowered his head. His mouth sought and found hers and this time she could not hold back her response as it clamoured to the fore. She swayed against him and instantly his arms closed like steel bands about her. 'Don't think,' Matthew had said. 'Make the most of this moment.' This was the easiest instruction she had ever had to follow, Tessa realised as she slid her arms about his neck and succumbed to the warmth of his kisses with a sort of bittersweet joy.

His lips strayed across her cheek, hovered for a moment where a pulse raced madly in the hollow of her throat, and then returned to her waiting lips. What did it matter if he was merely seeking forgetfulness in her arms, she thought ecstatically. This moment was hers to dream of and remember even if these kisses were intended for someone else, or with someone else in mind.

It seemed like an eternity before he released her and Tessa emerged from her dreamy state of bliss to face the stinging reality of the truth. It was over! It could never be recaptured now, after taking one look at the closed expression in his eyes, she knew that he must realise this as well.

'Goodnight, Tessa,' he said quietly. 'Sleep well.'

With a mumbled response she fled from the kitchen, an aching emptiness in her numbed heart, and longing so fierce that it seemed to tear her apart in its intensity. She meant nothing to Matthew and never could, not after loving someone as vivaciously lovely as Angela Sinclair. Not even Theresa Ashton-Smythe could compare or compete with such loveliness.

Tessa undressed in the darkness and slipped into bed, but sleep evaded her for some time as her mind leapt frantically from one thought to the other without much clarity. Tiredness made her incoherent and unable to see the situation in its proper perspective. Perhaps in the morning, she decided, perhaps then she would reach a sensible solution to this insurmountable problem.

CHAPTER SEVEN

TESSA avoided Matthew as much as possible during the next few days and rarely saw him, except at meal times. His attitude, since the evening of Barry's birthday party, was one of unapproachability. His behaviour towards Mrs Craig and Barry was not unfriendly, but Tessa was subjected to a chilly politeness that merely confirmed her suspicions that he considered the interlude between them as nothing more than a mere escape from reality on his part, and he probably hated himself for his momentary weakness.

'I'm worried about Matthew,' Mrs Craig announced one evening after dinner when they were alone in the living-room. Tessa had been playing the piano at Mrs Craig's request and now, as her employer spoke, she closed the lid of the piano and returned to her chair. 'When Matthew becomes silently morose,' Mrs Craig continued, 'he usually has something on his mind, and it's obviously something that's troubling him greatly. Do you perhaps know what it could be, Tessa?'

Tessa felt herself stiffen. 'Matthew isn't in the habit of confiding in me.'

'Matthew is not in the habit of confiding in anyone, but I thought that you may have noticed something which I'd missed.' Ethel Craig's glance was troubled. 'Do you think it has something to do with Angela?'

'I ... think it may have,' Tessa admitted hesitantly, her heart being ripped to shreds within her. 'I think he

124

loved her more than any of you realised, and that it was a blow to him to discover where her affections really lay. This was made very obvious the other evening by the way she and Barry hardly left each other's side.'

Mrs Craig picked up her work and continued her knitting in thoughtful silence, the needles flashing at regular intervals as they were caught in the light. 'You know, Tessa,' she said suddenly, dropping her knitting on to her lap, 'despite what you've said, I'm beginning to get the strangest feeling that he was never in love with Angela.'

'What makes you think that?' Tessa asked abruptly.

'Matthew is not the kind of person who would sit back calmly while allowing someone to snap up the thing he wants from right under his nose. No,' she shook her head firmly, 'he would have put up a fight for her affections, I'm certain.'

Tessa did not agree with this new theory of Mrs Craig's, but she was really in no position to enter a debate on the subject of whether or not Matthew Craig did love Angela Sinclair. It was painful enough knowing that she would never stand a chance to win his love, without discussing the validity of his personal feelings for another woman.

'Where is Matthew now?' Mrs Craig wanted to know as she resumed her knitting.

'In his study,' Tessa sighed heavily, 'where he always is lately.'

Not that she minded, she told herself, for while he was there she had no fear of running into him around every corner. 'But part of you is there with him all the same,' her conscience reminded her, and she admitted guiltily to herself that she *did* wonder continuously what he was doing, and longed unashamedly to be with him.

'Make us a pot of tea, my dear,' Mrs Craig suggested eventually. 'I'm beginning to long for my bed.' Then, almost as an afterthought, she added, 'Take Matthew a cup of tea to his study, it might help to cheer him up.'

Tessa's heart lurched violently at the thought of confronting him alone in his study, but she nodded with outward calm and went through to the kitchen to do as Mrs Craig had asked. Her hands trembled as she set the tray. It was a long time since she had taken Matthew anything to drink when he was alone in his study. Would he not perhaps think that she was now making it an excuse to see him alone? Well, she would soon rid him of that theory, she decided firmly as she carried the tray through to the living-room.

'Matthew likes very little milk in his tea and two sugars,' Mrs Craig informed her as she poured the tea.

Tessa handed Mrs Craig her cup of tea and then, with hammering heart and much trepidation, she took Matthew's tea to his study. He answered her knock with an abrupt 'Yes', and Tessa sent up a brief prayer before opening the door and entering. He sat there, surrounded by important-looking papers, a surprised expression on his face as she approached him.

'Your mother said I should bring you a cup of tea,' she explained hastily, placing the cup on his desk and turning to leave.

'Tessa!' he called as she reached the door, and she turned expectantly. For a brief second she thought he was going to speak to her, then his expression hardened

126

and he shook his head. 'It was nothing. You may go.'

Tessa felt curiously deflated as she returned to the living-room. What had he been about to say? she wondered distractedly. And what had made him change his mind? Oh, bother the man! she thought furiously. Why did she have to fall in love with *him*? Why could she not have had an uncomplicated relationship with the man she loved, like so many other girls? Why was it always so difficult for her to find the happiness she desired?

In a wave of self-pity she sat down and drank her tea before accompanying Mrs Craig to her room. 'You're walking very nicely with that stick,' she remarked sincerely.

'Yes, I am,' her employer smiled delightedly, 'but it's still nice to know that you're here beside me if I should need you.'

'You're a fraud, Mrs Craig,' Tessa teased laughingly. 'You haven't really needed me since that day the cast was removed. You've become self-sufficient once more.'

There was guilt written all over the older woman's face. 'I admit that I don't need you any more the way I used to but, let us say I've grown accustomed to your companionship and I'm loath to let you go.' Her smile was childlike and appealing. 'Am I forgiven?'

Tessa hesitated only a moment before leaning over and planting a kiss on her employer's wrinkled cheek. 'I've loved working for you, for I, too, have enjoyed your company. I——' her voice broke slightly as tears threatened, 'I shall hate to leave.'

'Couldn't you stay longer?' Mrs Craig asked hopefully.

'My job here is practically redundant,' Tessa replied

adamantly. 'No, I must leave at the end of next week, if not sooner.'

'Oh, not sooner, Tessa,' Mrs Craig exclaimed anxiously. 'Not sooner, please?'

Tessa made no reply but busied herself instead with the running of Mrs Craig's bath water. Even though she wanted to, she knew she could not stay a day longer than was planned, not while she loved Matthew so desperately.

'Stay and chat a while,' Mrs Craig begged as Tessa made her comfortable against the pillows and straightened the sheets, a ritual which was hard to break even though her employer was quite capable of doing this for herself.

'Aren't you tired of talking to me yet?' Tessa teased, seating herself on the side of the bed.

'My dear Tessa, you seem to have such a vast amount of knowledge stored away in that brain of yours that I've never once tired of your company.' She caught hold of Tessa's hand and squeezed it. 'You'll make some lucky man a wonderful wife one day.'

You'll make some lucky man a wonderful wife one day! Those words reverberated through Tessa's mind and jabbed mercilessly at her already bruised heart. Some lucky man, but *not* Matthew. *Not Matthew*! the words mocked her, and if it could not be Matthew, there would be no one else *ever*!

'Is there someone special in your life, Tessa?'

Tessa considered this a moment and then decided that, amid all the lies she had been forced to tell, it could do no harm to admit the truth. 'Yes, there is.'

'Someone in Johannesburg?'

128

'No.'

'Someone I know?'

Tessa laughed nervously. 'That would be telling, wouldn't it?'

'Yes, I suppose so,' Mrs Craig admitted ruefully. 'Forgive an old woman for being so inquisitive.'

'Inquisitive about what?' Matthew demanded directly behind Tessa, and she started violently.

'It's none of your business,' Ethel reprimanded her eldest son, but the reprimand was laced with affection. 'You have a nasty habit of creeping up on people then popping up at the most unexpected times. It's not very nice, especially if one is having a private discussion.'

'What would you have me do?' he asked, seating himself on the other side of the bed, his lips twisting into a little smile that did not quite reach his eyes. 'Shall I get myself a bell, and ring it as far as I go as a warning to everyone that I'm approaching?'

'Don't be silly,' Mrs Craig laughed, taking his hand. 'I'm glad you've come out of your study for a while to talk to your old mother. You've neglected me lately.'

'I'm sorry, Mother. There's been a tremendous amount of paper work to wade through.' He turned then and glanced thoughtfully at Tessa. 'I don't suppose you know anything about typing?'

'As a matter of fact, I do.'

Matthew raised his eyebrows. 'Remarkable!'

'Be careful, Tessa,' Mrs Craig warned humorously. 'I have an idea he's going to put you to work.'

Matthew rubbed his chin thoughtfully. 'Mother is right—I have a dozen or more letters to get in the post. My handwriting is atrocious and my typing is limited to two fingers only. Would it be asking too much of you to type them for me in the morning?' He glanced apologetically at his mother. 'That is, if you won't be needing her for anything?'

Mrs Craig smiled at Tessa. 'If Tessa doesn't mind, then I have no objection.'

Tessa felt as if the walls were closing in on her as Matthew's questioning glance lingered on her face. 'Well?'

'I'll type those letters for you,' she managed eventually, lowering her glance to the floral pattern on Mrs Craig's eiderdown, and hoping fervently that he could not hear the heavy beating of her treacherous heart.

'Good, that's settled, then,' he said briskly. 'Come to my study after breakfast tomorrow morning. I'll show you where everything is and then leave you to it.'

With that he engaged his mother in conversation and simply ignored Tessa's presence, giving her the longed for opportunity to escape. In the hall she ran into Barry and he caught her arm to stop her flight.

'You always seem to be dashing about,' he laughed at her. 'Where's the fire this time?'

'As usual there is no fire,' she smiled at him. 'It's just my terrible haste to get outside and grab some fresh air.'

'My, you are a fresh air fiend, aren't you?' he laughed. Matthew's voice could be heard coming from Mrs Craig's room and Barry tilted his head in a listening attitude. 'Don't tell me you were running away from Matthew again?'

Tessa stepped out on to the patio and the cool night air brushed gently against her hot cheeks. Why was it always so difficult to relax when Matthew was around?

It seemed as though an invisible barrier had been erected between them, a barrier that had not crumbled even in those brief moments he had made casual love to her. No! She corrected herself fiercely, there had been nothing casual in the way he had made love to her. He had intended to deliberately and masterfully arouse her, perhaps to prove the power he wielded over her emotionally, and he had succeeded.

Barry followed Tessa out into the garden. 'When are you going to stop running away from Matthew? I told you once before that if you gave him just a little more encouragement, you'd have him eating out of your hand.'

Tessa laughed bitterly at that. 'Matthew would take encouragement from me as an invitation to flirt, or perhaps become his mistress.'

'Oh, Tessa,' Barry shook his head sadly. 'You wouldn't say that if you knew Matthew better.'

'No, I don't know Matthew,' she cried in anguish, 'but I do know that he doesn't think much of me. If he did, he wouldn't have——' She bit off the rest of her sentence and swallowed convulsively.

'Wouldn't have what?'

'Nothing.' She gestured vaguely as if to brush aside her distasteful thoughts, and quickened her pace unconsciously. The garden was always so beautiful at night when it was bathed in moonlight, but Tessa was too disturbed to notice anything at that moment except her own vulnerability.

Barry caught hold of her arm. 'Slow down, Tessa, I have no intention of jogging round the garden with you.'

'I'm sorry.'

For a time they walked in silence and the scented peacefulness of the garden surrounded them. 'Tessa, I'd like to ask you a question,' Barry said suddenly, 'and I would like an honest reply. Are you in love with Matthew?'

A quiver ran through the length of her slender frame. 'Yes. Is it ... so obvious?'

'To me, yes, but I don't think anyone else has noticed,' he reassured her quickly, and Tessa relaxed once more. 'There's something else I've noticed as well,' Barry continued thoughtfully. 'Matthew has been spending more time up at the house than ever before lately. Does this have any significance for you?'

'Yes, it does,' she sighed heavily. 'He's checking up on me to see that I don't vanish with the family silver.'

'Don't be silly, I've seen the way he looks at you.'

'So have I,' Tessa remarked stiffly, the tears jerking at her throat. 'With mockery and suspicion.'

'There you go sticking your head in the sand again like an ostrich,' Barry reprimanded as he drew her down beside him on the garden bench. 'I remember once when we were kids there was a young pup in the pet shop in Idwala. Matthew wanted father to buy it for him, but Father insisted that there were enough dogs on the farm. Matthew and I spent the rest of that morning in the shop and he did nothing but sit and stare at that pup with that incredible, hopeless longing in his eyes.'

Tessa felt as though she would suffocate, the way her heart was beating in her throat. 'Why are you telling me this?'

'That's the way he looks at you.'

Hope fluttered bravely in her heart but she crushed it ruthlessly. Barry was wrong. Matthew desired her, perhaps, but desire was not love. If he loved her, why had he not said so on the night of Barry's party? Heaven knows she had given him enough indication as to the extent of her feelings by returning his fiery kisses with a passion that matched his own. 'Oh, God!' she groaned inwardly, 'how I loathe myself for allowing him to penetrate my defences! I longed for his arms and his kisses, but not for the reason he obviously chose to think.'

'Tessa?'

She snapped out of her unhappy reverie to stare long and hard at Barry's dark shape beside her on the bench. 'If you don't mind, I don't think I want to discuss this subject further. Tell me rather about yourself and Angela.

'Ah, yes,' he sighed agreeably. 'I do have some news for you. Angela has agreed to marry me.'

A ridiculous surge of joy swept through Tessa. 'Barry, I'm so happy for you both. When is the engagement to be announced?'

Barry grinned sheepishly. 'Well, we did think of announcing it this coming Saturday. I thought of inviting her parents along to dinner that evening so we could all celebrate together.'

Tessa frowned suddenly. 'Does you mother know? And Matthew ... has he any idea?'

'Not yet,' Barry admitted, oblivious of her concern. 'I'll tell Mother this evening when I go in to say goodnight, and then I shall have to confront Matthew with the news.'

133

'How—how do you think he'll take the news?' she asked lamely.

'I think he'll take it perfectly well,' Barry replied confidently, 'considering that his interests lie elsewhere.'

Tessa avoided his meaningful glance. 'Don't start that again!'

'No, I won't,' he agreed, taking her hand and pulling her to her feet. 'Let's go in so I can get it over with.'

Tessa left Barry at the door to his mother's room before going to her own. He seemed to spend a long time with her, for it was past ten when she heard him emerge and walk along the passage to Matthew's study, and her nerves tightened at the thought of what might follow.

She pulled on her gown and slippers and went along to Mrs Craig's room as she usually did before retiring, but on this occasion she felt a sense of guilt at this perfectly natural errand, as though her employer might think she had come out of curiosity. Shrugging her shoulders at the thought, she opened the door to Mrs Craig's room some moments later and entered.

A glowing smile greeted her as she came towards the bed. 'Barry has just given be the most wonderful news, and I'm so happy that I feel like celebrating at this very moment.'

It all came tumbling out and Tessa could only stand and stare at the happiness shining so beautifully on the face of the woman she had come to care for.

'My ultimate joy will now be to see Matthew happily married,' she ended off on a little note of sadness that found an echo in Tessa's heart. 'Do you think we could celebrate with a glass of cocoa?'

'I'll go and make some,' Tessa smiled down into mischievous green eyes and left the room.

In passing Matthew's study she heard the murmur of voices from within and paused a moment, wondering how Matthew was taking the news of Barry's forthcoming engagement to Angela. One consoling thought was that they were at least not shouting at each other. Footsteps sounded close to the door and Tessa hastily headed for the kitchen before she was discovered and accused of attempting to eavesdrop. She had already warmed the milk when slow, heavy footsteps came towards the kitchen.

Matthew! her wild beating heart told her, and her hands trembled uncontrollably as she removed the milk from the stove, striving towards outward calmness at least.

'Making cocoa?' he asked directly behind her, causing nervous little tremors to run up her spine.

'Yes, would you like some?'

'Yes, please, if it's not too much trouble.'

The hint of mockery in his voice hurt and angered her simultaneously as she swung round to face him, her blue eyes flashing. 'I wouldn't have offered if I thought it would be too much trouble.'

To her consternation his green eyes slid down the length of her to her slipper-clad feet before sweeping upwards again. Her cheeks reddened and involuntarily her hands tightened the belt of her gown. He was suddenly his old mocking self, and she wondered miserably whether Barry's news had brought about this change in him.

'Has anyone ever told you that you're beautiful when

you're angry, and absolutely enchanting when you blush?' he asked.

In confusion and embarrassment Tessa stared up at him, but she was not to be outdone. 'Has anyone ever told you that you're insufferable?'

For a moment she thought she had gone too far as she noticed his eyes darkening, then, strangely, he seemed to find the situation amusing.

'If you're going to make cocoa, I suggest you do so before the milk gets cold,' he mocked her, and Tessa felt as though she could throw something at him.

The atmosphere was strained as she made the cocoa and handed him his mug in angry silence, while taking great care to avoid his eyes.

'I suppose you've heard the news about Barry and Angela?' he asked casually, and only then did she raise her glance swiftly to his, but his expression betrayed nothing to convey his feelings.

'Yes, I have,' she informed him, forcing as much casualness into her own voice as she could muster.

'It's about time Barry settled down, and Angela is just the girl to make him happy. They're ideally suited,' he added, sipping at his cocoa and meeting her look of total disbelief over the rim of his mug.

'You don't mind?'

'Is there any reason why I should?'

Her hands fluttered nervously. 'Well, I—I thought——'

'That I was in love with Angela?' he finished for her, his lips twisting cynically into a smile that displayed strong white teeth.

'Well ... yes,' she admitted, feeling utterly foolish and slightly stunned.

A brief silence hung ominously in the air between them until he said, 'Well, I'm sorry I have to disappoint you, and that I have no broken heart to produce for your inspection.'

Tessa drew her breath in sharply at the cynicism in his voice. 'I didn't presume you'd be broken hearted, in fact I'm certain that's something you'll never be.'

'Really?' he drawled curiously, his eyes narrowed. 'What makes you say that?'

Tessa took a deep breath to steady her nerves and plunged in feet first. 'You're far too arrogant and cynical to ever fall in love in the first place, and therefore you won't ever suffer from a broken heart, if you have such a thing as a heart, for I'm certain that a cold slab of concrete has lodged in its place.'

Without looking at him she picked up the tray and headed towards the door, only to find her path blocked by a dangerously transformed Matthew. His face was dark with anger, his eyes like two coals of fire searing through her, while the muscles in his jaw seemed to ripple with the effort of self-control. She was frightened, more frightened than she had ever been in her life, and she had only herself to blame for this.

'Put down that tray,' he commanded through his clenched teeth.

'Your mother is waiting for her cocoa,' she tried to evade him anxiously, but he repeated his command and Tessa knew that there was nothing else she could do but obey.

Matthew closed the kitchen door and advanced upon her. She stepped back in an effort to escape, but his arms shot out and his fingers bit cruelly into her shoulders as he pulled her against him ruthlessly. Tessa

137

struggled against him, but her puny efforts were futile for his arms merely tightened about her like a vice.

'You went too far this time, Tessa,' he said harshly, his face inches from her own and distorted with the most terrible anger.

'Matthew, please!' she begged gaspingly. 'I—I didn't mean——'

'Oh, yes, you did! You meant every word, and now you'll pay for them.'

'No, no, let me go! Please!'

Her cries were stifled as his mouth claimed hers ruthlessly in a form of punishment more painful than she had ever experienced. Every part of her being resisted this onslaught until his technique altered swiftly and subtly. He forced her lips apart with his own and kissed her with a drowning sensuality she could not fight against. She had lost and he knew it, for she could feel the confidence in his touch as he pushed her gown aside to bury his lips against the creamy warmth of her shoulder.

'So I have no heart, have I?' he muttered against her neck, and Tessa crashed down to earth with a thud.

'This has nothing to do with the heart, or loving, Matthew,' she managed eventually, struggling to free herself. 'This is nothing more than animal desire.'

'Perhaps, but desire can be a wonderful substitute,' he said moving his hands possessively over her hips and drawing her closer to the lean hardness of his body. 'Don't you agree?'

Tessa trembled at his touch and experienced several other emotions that eventually brought a swift rush of tears to her eyes, and they were tears of anger, frustration and disappointment. His eyes were mocking her and a strange new coldness settled about her heart that drove all other emotions from it.

'Please, let me go, Matthew,' she said in a voice that was now equally cold and, to her surprise, he did as she asked. 'W-would you mind t-taking your mother's cocoa to her?' she asked him before wrenching open the door and escaping.

Alone in the darkness of her small room, Tessa lay in a crumpled heap across her bed and cried until the tears ceased to flow, but her indulgence in this form of weakness did nothing to lighten the burden of her conscience. She rolled over on to her back and stared into the darkness with eyes that were red and swollen from weeping. The situation had become intolerable and there was only one thing she could do. She would have to leave, and soon.

She had come into this house under false pretences, aided and abetted by Mrs Craig, who had insisted she should pretend to be the substitute for the unknown Miss Emmerson who had been unable to come at the last minute. Added to this was her own deceit by using a false name. What had started out as a harmless venture, would end in a fiasco if she did not leave immediately.

Barry, bless him, had insinuated that Matthew might care for her, but Barry had merely been kind, of this she was certain, for Matthew still harboured his original opinion of her. She could, of course, go to Matthew and tell him the truth. He would be angered by her deceit, but it might mean that their relationship could perhaps continue on a better level. Tessa pummelled her pillow angrily. This idea would put paid to her desire to be loved for herself. Perhaps she was being foolish, but there had to be no doubt in her mind on this subject.

She toyed with this idea for some time before dispelling it. Barry's suggestion that Matthew cared for her was ludicrous, considering his behaviour towards her, but ... she could not help lingering on this thought ... if it were true, would he not be even angrier at discovering her true identity?

She slipped off the bed and paced the floor restlessly. Matthew would hate the knowledge that he had been deceived and, even if he could bring himself to care for her, she had no doubt that he would not hesitate in sending her packing, regardless of his own feelings.

Whichever way Tessa looked at it, she was on the losing side, and there was only one avenue left open to her. She would have to leave as soon as she could despite the fact that, for the rest of her life, she would have to live with the knowledge that the man she loved did not care.

CHAPTER EIGHT

SLEEP evaded Tessa that night, and she started the day with a blinding headache and dark smudges beneath her eyes as further evidence of her restless night. She hated the idea of having to face Matthew that morning, but there was no way of avoiding the meeting since she had agreed to type those letters for him.

With a sigh she threw aside the blankets, then bathed and changed into a comfortable pair of beige slacks and cherry-coloured shirt, in the hope that it would brighten her appearance. She creamed her face before putting on her make-up and brushing her hair, then, standing back to inspect herself, she grimaced at the evidence of her sleepless night which had been unable to camouflage successfully. She dabbed a little more powder beneath her eyes and decided it would have to suffice under the circumstances.

She had not quite finished preparing the breakfast when Matthew walked into the kitchen. He looked surprisingly young in his blue denim shirt and slacks, with comfortable suede shoes. After a brief greeting, Tessa tried to ignore him but, as always, Matthew made his presence felt by coming up behind her to peer over her shoulder at what she was doing.

'That bacon smells delicious,' he remarked, sniffing ostentatiously. 'I didn't realise how hungry I was.'

How on earth did he manage to remain so cool and unaffected after what had occurred between them? she

141

wondered, and not without a touch of resentment.

'If you'll sit down I'll serve your breakfast,' she said curtly as she scooped the eggs and bacon into his plate.

Matthew had barely started eating when Barry breezed in. He rubbed his hands together before patting his stomach. 'Gosh, I'm hungry.'

'You're *always* hungry,' Tessa rebuked playfully, his presence alleviating some of the tension.

'Can I help it if I'm a growing boy who needs lots of food?' he teased ruefully, seating himself at the table.

'You're no longer a boy, and the only direction you'll grow in is in the outward direction.'

'Are you telling me that I'm fat?' Barry asked with mock severity.

'No,' Tessa laughed, 'but you will be if you're not careful.'

Matthew ignored their raillery. 'Don't forget that I shall be expecting you in my study the moment you've had your own breakfast,' he reminded her as she prepared to leave with Mrs Craig's breakfast tray.

'I shan't forget.'

How could she forget? she asked herself as she went down the passage. The very thought of having to be alone with him in his study was enough to fill her with dread, but if he could play it cool, then so could she, she decided defiantly.

'Forgive me for saying this,' Mrs Craig remarked in amusement, 'but you have the appearance of someone preparing for battle.'

Tessa relaxed visibly and managed a tight laugh at the astuteness of her employer. 'Perhaps I *am* preparing for battle. Who knows?'

Her vague reply did not perturb Mrs Craig and Tessa, after making her comfortable, returned to the kitchen to have her own meal. She was too nervous to eat and finally settled for a slice of toast and a cup of coffee. Daisy entered the kitchen at that moment and Tessa, not wanting to keep Matthew waiting, asked her to give Mrs Craig some assistance if she should require it.

When Tessa entered Matthew's study, she found him standing at the window staring out across the valley, and she was very aware of his broad shoulders, slim hips, and muscular thighs. He turned then and Tessa averted her glance quickly.

'I apologise for encroaching upon you in this way,' he said, coming towards her, 'but I shall certainly be grateful for your help.'

He sounded almost human, she marvelled to herself with a touch of cynicism. 'Show me what you want done and I'll do my best.'

Matthew gestured towards his desk. 'I put the type-writer here because I thought it might give you more space to work. If the chair isn't high enough you could swivel it around until it's the height you require.' He pointed to a wad of typing paper and carbon. 'I think that should be enough, don't you?'

'More than enough,' she assured him tritely, clasping her hands together in front of her to stop their nervous fluttering.

Matthew handed her several sheafs of paper on which he had written the letters that required typing. 'I hope you'll be able to read my handwriting.'

Tessa glanced down at them, reading a few passages

143

here and there. His handwriting was firm and large, like most men, but with a distinctive touch of arrogance in the curve of some of the letters. 'I'll manage.'

Matthew regarded her in silence for several seconds that seemed more like an eternity until a hot wave of discomfort enveloped her. 'You have smudges beneath your eyes. Aren't you feeling well?'

'I ... have a slight headache,' she replied, her voice quivering slightly as she averted her glance and minimised the stabbing pain which had settled between her eyes.

'Have you taken something for it?'

'No, I—I'll take something later.'

To her surprise she heard water being poured into a glass, then he brushed past her and opened one of the desk drawers, extracting a bottle of tablets. He unscrewed the cap and dropped two into the palm of his hand.

'Take these,' he said quietly, his hand brushing hers lightly as he handed her the tablets. 'The water is there beside you on the desk.'

Consideration from Matthew was something quite unusual for Tessa and for a moment she stared at him stupidly.

'You want to get rid of your headache, don't you?' he asked with a touch of exasperation in his deep voice.

'Yes ... yes, of course.'

'Then take those tablets.' His glance had a touch of the old mockery in it. 'It's nothing lethal, I can assure you.'

Tessa could not prevent the smile that quivered on her lips. 'I didn't think it was,' she told him quickly, and swallowed the tablets before he could say anything further.

'Thank you,' she whispered as he took the empty glass from her and replaced it on the small cupboard in the corner. 'You're very kind.'

'I wasn't being kind,' he observed easily. 'I merely wanted to make sure that your headache wouldn't prevent you from typing those letters for me.'

This was too much for Tessa, and her anger rose sharply despite the fact that she sensed he was merely teasing her. Unable to prevent herself, she turned on him and released some of her pent-up emotions in a flurry of words that could have remained unsaid. 'I should have known that you never do anything without having an ulterior motive. I said you were kind, but I was wrong. You haven't one shred of kindness in you, so you wouldn't know how if you tried. You're the most arrogant, self-centred, egotistical man I've ever had the misfortune to meet, and I hope I shall never see you again once I've left here!'

The silence following her outburst was heavily charged, and one glance at the cold expression in Matthew's eyes was enough to bring her to her senses. Her hand flew to her throat where a nerve throbbed painfully and, to her horror, she realised that she was close to tears.

'I'm sorry,' she whispered, distraught, lowering her glance to the tanned column of his throat. 'My head aches, I didn't sleep very well, and I didn't really mean all those things I've just said.'

Again there was silence, then she saw his broad chest heave slightly. 'I shall accept your apology for what it's worth,' he said, his deep voice vibrating along her already tender nerves and, without another word, he turned and left her alone in his study.

Three hours later Tessa arched her aching back and placed the cover on the typewriter. She arranged Matthew's letters into a neat pile on his desk and went in search of Mrs Craig. She had gone over in her mind so many times what she wanted to say, but each time she had discarded her little speech in preference of another. Perhaps it would be more sensible to let it all come out quite naturally and without all the pleasant little clichés she had thought up.

She found Ethel Craig on the patio having tea, and the way the older woman's face brightened at the sight of her gave a twist to her heart that almost made her change her mind.

'You're just in time for tea,' Mrs Craig informed her brightly. 'I told Daisy to delay the tea in the hope that you would be able to join me. It's such a lovely day, and it's an absolute shame that you've had to sit cooped up in that study for so long.'

'Well, I shan't have to return to it, as I have finished Matthew's letters,' Tessa told her while she poured herself a cup of tea. 'My time is all yours.'

'You may not believe this, Tessa,' Mrs Craig began after a brief silence, 'but I've grown exceptionally fond of you.'

'And I of you,' Tessa replied truthfully.

'I wish there was some way I could keep you here.'

Miraculously, this was Tessa's cue and, closing her mind and heart to all but her objective, she plunged

146

into speech. 'Mrs Craig, I've loved working for you and I'm going to miss you dreadfully, but I would like you to release me from your employ as from tomorrow.' She bit her lip at the look of dismay on Mrs Craig's face. 'I know this is sudden and that you asked me to—to stay until the end of next week, but I—I must leave before —before ...' She could not continue and stared miserably down at the stone paving.

'Why must you leave, Tessa?' her employer asked quietly. 'Can't you tell me?'

Tears were brimming Tessa's eyes and hovering on her eyelashes. 'Mrs Craig, I got this job with you under false pretences.'

'Yes, my dear, I know. We indulged in a little deception by saying that you were Miss Emmerson's replacement.' She observed Tessa closely. 'Surely this isn't troubling you?'

Tessa shook her head and took a deep breath. 'I'm afraid my deception is far greater than that.'

'Are you referring to the fact that you are Theresa Ashton-Smythe and not Tessa Smith?'

Tessa drew her breath in sharply, her bewildered glance searching Mrs Craig's calm features. 'You know?'

A gentle smile touched the older woman's lips. 'I've known from the very beginning.'

'But—but——' Tessa stared at her incredulously. 'How did you know? And why didn't you say so?'

Ethel Craig laughed softly and poured herself another cup of tea. 'You forget, my dear, that being confined to a wheelchair gave me many hours during which I had to find something to occupy myself with.

147

I read everything I could lay my hands on, and it so happened that I was going through an old batch of magazines I've never managed to read previously. It was in one of those magazines that I read an article about your forthcoming wedding. That should give you some idea how old those magazines were.' She sipped at her tea. 'I must admit that at first you had me fooled with your short hair and unflattering clothes, but underneath it was Theresa Ashton-Smythe all right. You arrived here at a most opportune moment, and I immediately thought up the idea of putting you forward as Miss Emmerson's replacement.'

'But why?' Tessa asked, still bewildered.

Once again that smile touched Mrs Craig's lips. 'You gave your name as Tessa Smith, remember? I knew then that you were either escaping from something or that life itself had driven you to the point where you had to seek anonymity.' Her glance was gently probing. 'Which was it, Tessa?'

Tessa felt relief at the prospect of being able to confide in Mrs Craig, and she did so, omitting nothing.

'My marriage to Jeremy Fletcher never materialised. I was jilted. He sent me a cryptic little letter in which he told me that he was marrying someone else whom he loved, and that his only reason for wanting to marry me had been for financial gain. This, to me, had been a stunning blow that was to have far-reaching effects.' Tessa ran her fingers along the arm of the cane chair as she allowed her thoughts to drift back over the past twenty-two months. 'I was studying music at the university and I had another year to go, which I would have completed after my marriage. Shortly after every-

148

thing fell through, I received an unexpected offer to study in Europe, and I jumped at the chance to get away. My parents naturally agreed that a change of surroundings would perhaps be ideal for me, emotionally. I spent a year in Europe before returning to South Africa with the intention of starting a school of music, but I found instead that I was giving recitals, something I didn't care for very much. Mother wanted me to be a concert pianist and my father went along with the idea, but basically they didn't care very much as long as I was happy.'

She rose to her feet then, unable to sit still a moment longer. She paced about restlessly while continuing her story. 'I have many friends, Mrs Craig, and I'm very fond of them all, but Jeremy sowed a seed of doubt in my mind which I found difficult to eradicate. I was becoming cynical, trusting no one, and finally I started wondering how many of my friends were actually my friends because they really liked me. I began to doubt their sincerity, and I think they were beginning to suspect that something was amiss.'

'I can understand this,' Mrs Craig remarked with understanding. 'You wanted to be liked for yourself, and not for who you are.'

'Yes,' Tessa nodded briefly before continuing her story. 'One evening, after a particularly gruelling recital, I attended a party to celebrate the success of the evening. To my surprise, Jeremy and his wife were there as well. We greeted each other like civilised human beings, he introduced me to his wife, and then we spent the rest of the evening avoiding each other. There was nothing left of my feelings for him, but I

149

couldn't help remembering that he had intended marrying me for my money. The thought filled me with revulsion, and it was then that I decided to get away from it all to find myself, as it were, and to discover whether people could accept me as their friend when I was ordinary Tessa Smith.'

'Your parents didn't object to this idea of yours?'

'No,' Tessa smiled. 'They were concerned for my safety, of course, but they fortunately understood. I decided to tour the country in order to meet new people and see new faces. Just being Miss Smith was going to be fun. Unfortunately, I lost my way and had to call on here to ask directions to the nearest town. I was taken for the new housekeeper/companion and found myself with a job before I could refuse.' Tessa laughed tremulously. 'The rest you know.'

Ethel Craig's glance was apologetic. 'I must admit that I did push you into this position rather unceremoniously. 'I'm not normally an impulsive person, but I sensed that something was making you unhappy and I wanted to help you.'

Tessa knelt down in front of her chair and took her hands in her own. 'You've been very kind to me, Mrs Craig.'

'There's just one matter I wish to stress.' The hands clasping Tessa's tightened. 'Knowing your true identity made no difference to the way I feel about you. I like you, Tessa, and getting to know you has been a revelation. Wealth and success has not spoiled you. You're warm and sincere and there is an enormous amount of love locked away in your heart for someone lucky enough to find the key. You have proved that no task is too menial for you, and I must admit that there were times when I dreaded the thought of your lovely hands being ruined by housework.' She turned Tessa's hands over and examined them carefully. 'I thank God that they've survived. Why are you crying?'

Tessa made no effort to hide the tears that were running freely down her cheeks. 'I'm crying because, for the first time in my life, I feel as though I've acquired a real friend, and I shall hate leaving here. I—I've found happiness here with you.' And love, her heart cried. 'I must go, Mrs Craig. I daren't stay a day longer.'

'But why not?'

Tessa swallowed convulsively. 'If Matthew discovered the truth about me, he would never forgive me. I must go before he finds out.'

Mrs Craig glanced down at her speculatively in a moment of lingering silence. 'If it matters so much what Matthew thinks of you, are you actually prepared to admit defeat without even putting up a fight?'

Tessa marvelled at the woman's astuteness. 'I see now that it's futile trying to hide anything from you, so I may as well admit that I've fallen hopelessly in love with that impossible son of yours.'

A satisfied little smile curved Ethel Craig's lips. 'Are you going to disappoint me by running away?'

'I can't accept your challenge,' Tessa whispered unhappily. 'Matthew doesn't love me.'

'Are you sure?'

Tessa rose to her feet then and walked about restlessly once more. Was she sure? No, she was too confused to be sure of anything. Matthew had given no indication whatsoever that he cared. The times he had made love to her had been purely to test her reaction, and to confirm his suspicions about her morality, had it not? Could she have misinterpreted his actions? she wondered seriously as she stared out across the garden. Oh, if only she knew!

Tessa had extracted a promise of silence from Mrs Craig on condition that she remained on the farm until the end of the following week. Mrs Craig had laughingly called it 'gentle blackmail', and Tessa could not refuse. As far as Matthew was concerned, Tessa remained a coward and avoided him as much as possible during the next few days.

Angela and her parents had been invited to dinner on the Saturday evening for the official announcement of Barry and Angela's engagement, and Tessa kept herself occupied most of that morning and part of the afternoon with the preparations. Finding eventually that she had an hour to herself, Tessa indulged in her favourite pastime by wandering through the garden in an attempt to rid herself of the disturbing thoughts which continually haunted her.

'That's a crane flower, also known as the Bird of Paradise,' Matthew spoke suddenly behind her as she stopped to examine a flower. She had not heard him approach.

'I thought this plant was called a strelitzia,' she remarked mischievously.

'If you must have the complete botanical name,' he said, 'it's a strelitzia reginae.'

Tessa raised her eyebrows in mocking surprise. 'I didn't realise that you were so well informed,' she said.

'Perhaps because you've never bother to find out anything about me.'

His green eyes regarded her steadily. As always, she and Matthew were beginning to spar with each other, and Tessa was in no mood to do verbal or physical battle with him. 'Yes—well, I—I must go.'

'Running away again?' he said.

'And what's that supposed to mean?' she demanded angrily.

'Oh, come now, Tessa,' he laughed derisively. 'You've been avoiding me lately as though I have a contagious disease or something. Every time I walk into a room, you rush out. It's getting beyond the funny stage, I can tell you.'

'I wasn't aware of the fact that you particularly yearned for my company,' she snapped back. 'Unfortunately I have work to do, so if you'll excuse me——'

His fingers closed about her wrist in an agonising grip. 'Let me go, you're hurting me!'

'Stop running away from me, Tessa,' he insisted calmly, slackening his hold but not releasing her.

'I'm not running away from you,' she flared hotly. 'Now will you please let me go!'

Matthew stared at her thoughtfully for a moment and then, surprisingly, he released her, his glance shifting to something beyond her. 'By the way,' he said quietly, 'there's a snake behind you.'

'No!' she screamed in absolute terror as she flew into the safety of his waiting arms like a homing pigeon. 'Where is it?' she asked, glancing nervously over her shoulder.

'There wasn't a snake,' he grinned, holding her

153

tightly, 'but the idea of one seems to have worked well.'

'You beast!' she cried, pummelling his chest in an effort to escape. 'That was a foul thing to do, and I hate you!'

'Do you hate me?' he asked softly, lowering his head and sliding his lips along the column of her throat to where a pulse leapt madly at his touch. 'Do you really hate me?'

'I—I—Oh, Matthew, please don't,' she begged weakly as her resistance deserted her.

She made a last futile effort to free herself, and in a moment she found herself crushed so fiercely against him that she expected her ribs to crack at any moment. He kissed her again and again until she hung limply in his arms, frightened by the intensity of his kisses, yet almost begging for more.

'We can't go on like this, Tessa,' he said suddenly. 'The situation has become intolerable.'

'W-what has become intolerable?' she stammered nervously.

'Me wanting you, and you for ever running away from me.'

His bluntness shocked her to her senses. 'What do you suggest we do about it?' she asked guardedly.

Matthew's eyes swept over her. 'I suggest that we admit our need of each other and let things go on from there.'

Tessa felt as though he had thrown a douche of cold water in her face as she stared at him in silence. 'Are you suggesting,' she asked awkwardly, an aching void where her heart ought to be, 'that I become your mistress?'

'For God's sake, Tessa, what kind of man do you think I am?'

She gestured helplessly with her hands, almost pleadingly. 'What do you expect me to think?' she cried in anguish. 'You talk of wanting me, and of admitting our need of each other. How else am I supposed to interpret your words?'

Matthew raked his fingers through his hair. It was a habit of his, she had noticed, when he was exasperated. 'Why can't you understand what I'm trying to say? At the moment we're going round in circles and getting nowhere!' he almost shouted at her, and Tessa flinched as she backed away from him.

'Exactly where are we supposed to be going?'

'Tessa, I'm trying very hard to make you realise that I love you, but you will persist in twisting everything I say out of proportion.'

Matthew continued reprimanding her, but Tessa no longer heard. The most exquisite joy surged through her, sending her heartbeat soaring and leaving her weak with the unbelievable knowledge that he loved her after all.

'You're always avoiding me,' Matthew continued. 'Whenever I come near you, you're quick to find something to do elsewhere.'

Tessa felt as though her heart would never quite resume its normal pace. 'Matthew, my darling, when are you going to stop talking, and kiss me?'

He stared at her for a moment, then he caught her in his arms, and Tessa offered no resistance as his lips claimed hers.

'Oh, Matthew,' she sighed some time later as she

pressed close against him. 'Why didn't you tell me ages ago that you loved me? Why did you let me go on thinking that you were just amusing yourself with me?'

'You weren't exactly oncoming,' he told her, sliding his hands down the hollow of her back and sending delicious tremors up her spine.

'You can't say that I offered much resistance the night of Barry's birthday party,' she reminded him.

He slid a finger beneath her chin and tilted her face upwards. 'Despite the fact that I doubted you, I couldn't resist making love to you a little.'

'Are you sure of me now?'

'I shall be when you tell me you love me.' His glance was questioning. 'Do you?'

'Yes. Oh, yes,' she assured him breathlessly, for the first time offering her lips of her own accord. She slid her arms about his waist and pressed closer to him, moving her hands caressingly over his muscular back.

'Don't do that,' he almost groaned, tearing his lips from hers and holding her a little distance away from him to look down into her flushed face. 'You're beautiful, Tessa, and I love you very much.'

'I can't believe you love me,' Tessa remarked dreamily as they strolled back to the house. 'I thought you were in love with Angela.'

Matthew pressed her closer to his side. 'I never loved Angela. The only reason I kept bringing her home was because I was hoping Barry would take an interest. She suits him well, don't you think?'

'You're a sly old fox,' she laughed up at him, marvelling at the thought that she could be so natural with him now that she was certain of his love.

The only thing that marred her moment of happiness was the fact that she still had to confide in Matthew, as she had done to his mother. 'Not now,' her heart cried, 'not yet!' and Tessa agreed. This moment was too heavenly to shatter with a confession, especially the kind of confession she had to make. She needed a little more time, she told herself, to adjust to the newness of this situation before she confronted Matthew with the truth. He would be angry, she knew, but it was a risk she would have to take, and she could only hope that he would eventually understand.

On the patio he drew her against him once more and kissed her hard on the mouth. 'You were far from me in thought for a moment. What were you thinking of?'

Tessa traced his firm lip with a loving finger. 'I was thinking of you. From the moment we met I've been able to think of no one else.'

There was a curious glint in his eyes as he replied, 'Despite the fact that my first thoughts of you weren't very charitable, I couldn't help loving you. I still don't know the mystery that surrounds you, but I don't care.'

Tessa's eyes filled with unexpected tears. 'That's the nicest thing you've ever said to me. I know I should clear up the mystery for you, but I'm frightened to spoil this moment of happiness.' She slid her arms about his neck and pushed her fingers through his fair hair. 'Will you be patient a little longer?'

'When you ask so prettily, how can I refuse?' He kissed her swiftly before they entered the house. 'Shall we keep our secret a little longer until after Barry's announcement this evening?'

Tessa agreed readily, not wanting to spoil anything

for Barry and revelling in the thought that she could savour the knowledge of their love in private for a little longer. The miracle had happened. Matthew loved her! He loved her for herself, and not because she was Theresa Ashton-Smythe, and this was what she had hoped for. The most difficult part was still to come before she could claim that his happiness was entirely hers. It was like a raging river that had to be crossed, and she knew that the crossing could not be delayed indefinitely.

CHAPTER NINE

TESSA did not see Matthew again until it was almost time for the Sinclair family to arrive. After making sure that everything was in order for the celebration dinner, she hurriedly bathed and changed. Mrs Craig had insisted that she could manage on her own, so Tessa had a few more minutes to herself and took more time than usual with her make-up. Her face had lost its pinched look and her eyes had acquired a glow which was not entirely due to the lighting in the room. This was what love could do for one, she thought as she stared at her reflection in the mirror. She looked almost radiant.

As she emerged from her room, she was delighted to see Matthew come striding down the passage towards her, dressed in a dark suit, white shirt and tie. It was the first time she had seen him dressed other than casually and her pulse rate quickened involuntarily. He reached her side swiftly and, before she realised his intentions, he had pushed her back into her room and closed the door. Her heart leapt to her throat as his arms closed about her.

'Matthew, you shouldn't be here in my room,' she protested, her voice muffled against his jacket. 'What if someone found us here together?'

'Can I help it if you come out into the passage looking absolutely delightful?' he whispered, kissing her in a way that sent fires of delight coursing through her veins. 'You haven't yet paid for those terrible names you called me the other day. Now what were they?' He raised his head thoughtfully, his face assuming a stern expression that did not frighten her at all. 'Oh, yes. Arrogant, self-centred and egotistical.'

'Matthew, I didn't really mean what I said,' she pleaded, realising that her own emotions were racing beyond the point of sanity as his hands moved caressingly down the hollow of her back and over her hips.

'Don't make excuses now that I have you cornered,' he laughed down at her, a glint in his eyes that made her quiver. 'Accept your punishment with good grace.'

Matthew's form of punishment was to make a gently sensual onslaught on emotions she tried so valiantly to keep in check, and Tessa was powerless to resist as her defences crumbled at the first charge. She allowed herself to be swept along on a tide of emotion until she felt the urgent pressure of his hand against her breast.

'Matthew darling, I—I love you, but we m-must go,' she gasped, her breath coming unevenly over parted lips that were still warm and unashamedly yearning for his kisses.

Reluctantly Matthew released her, his hands still lingering at her waist, their warm pressure not allowing the rapid beating of her heart to subside.

'I suppose Angela and her parents will be here any moment now,' he sighed, moving away from her and opening the door. 'I wish it was our engagement we were celebrating.'

'So do I,' Tessa echoed, her heart in her eyes, and Matthew would have swept her into his arms once more had she not successfully escaped him by darting past him into the passage.

Angela was a picture of loveliness that evening, her happiness draped about her like a glittering cloak, and Tessa had never seen Barry so calm and self-assured before. His behaviour was quite sober without the usual flippant remarks and he was ever attentive at Angela's side, holding her hand quietly at times, or merely passing a hand over her hair as he passed her chair.

Mr and Mrs Sinclair were a charming couple and they made no secret of the fact that they were extremely happy with their daughter's choice. There was no doubt that Mrs Craig, too, was exceptionally happy that Barry would finally be settling down, and with someone she approved of so completely.

Tessa's eyes met Matthew's across the room and the warmth in his glance sent the colour rushing into her cheeks. Oh, if only she had not entered into this foolish form of deceit, then this feeling of impending disaster would not be there to mar this moment of complete joy and happiness, she thought with a trace of bitterness.

Before dinner that evening, Barry opened the bottles of champagne and filled everyone's glasses. 'Ladies and gentlemen,' he began ceremoniously as they all stood waiting, 'we all know the reason for this small get-together, so let's not prolong the issue.' He drew Angela to his side. 'Angela has agreed to marry me, and we have her parents' blessing.'

'And mine,' Mrs Craig added happily.

'And yours, Mother,' Barry acknowledged smilingly. He placed his glass on the table and then placed Angela's beside his own before delving into his jacket pocket. He extracted a small velvet-covered box and flipped open the lid. 'This ring is beginning to burn a hole in my pocket, so let's put it where it belongs.'

He slid the ring on to Angela's finger and then, to everyone's delight, took her in his arms and kissed her soundly. They lifted their glasses and drank a toast to Barry and Angela's happiness, and then there was slight chaos as they all offered their personal congratulations and clamoured to see the ring, which was a beautiful solitaire diamond, set in a delicate gold setting.

'When is the wedding to be?' Tessa asked Angela after admiring her ring with an inexplicable feeling of envy in her heart, and a growing premonition of disaster.

'We haven't decided on a date yet,' Angela told her readily, 'but both Barry and I agree that a long engagement would be unbearable.'

'I don't want to give her too much time to change her mind,' Barry chipped in laughingly as he slipped an arm about her waist.

'Are you afraid I might have second thoughts, darling?' Angela teased.

'Not afraid, just cautious,' he admitted with an element of seriousness. 'Getting you to agree the first time was bad enough, I couldn't go through it a second time.'

'Shame! Poor darling,' Angela pouted playfully, patting his cheek and blowing him a kiss.

It was not until late that evening, after settling Mrs Craig for the night, that Tessa managed to have a few words with Matthew. But it appeared that Matthew, too, wished to speak with her, for he was waiting for her to emerge from his mother's room and, as she closed the door behind her, she went swiftly to his side. He cast her an icy glance that filled her with sudden dread. 'Come to my study. We can talk privately there.'

In silence Tessa followed him, and every step she took seemed to take her closer to something which could only spell her doom. There was only one thing she could think of that might have this alarming effect upon him. Her true identity! Had he found out? she wondered when they were finally alone in his study with the vast expanse of his desk between them.

Tessa faced him nervously, her eyes beseeching. 'Matthew, what's upset you? What's happened?'

Without a word, he slipped his hand into his jacket pocket and extracted a piece of paper which he handed to her. Tessa's hands shook as she stared down at the newspaper cutting. It was an old photograph of Jeremy and herself at one of her mother's charity functions, and the caption underneath referred to their coming marriage. A coldness seeped in under her skin that had a numbing effect upon her. There was only one way she could save the situation now, she decided, and that was to treat the whole matter calmly and matter-of-factly.

'It's not a very good likeness,' she said, allowing the cutting to flutter on to the desk.

'Then you don't deny that it's you?'

'What would be the use?'

'That's just as well,' he continued coldly. 'I searched your room while you were with Mother, and I found this.'

He flipped a cheque book across the desk at her. A cheque book with her name clearly printed at the bottom of each cheque. *T. Ashton-Smythe.*

Tessa had a peculiar feeling that a piece of lead had lodged in her heart as she met his accusing glance. 'I can explain, Matthew.'

'I'm sure you can,' he said cynically, gesturing towards the photograph. 'What happened to him?'

Tessa faced him unflinchingly. 'He married someone else.'

'Why?'

'He didn't really love me,' she whispered. 'He merely wanted to marry me for financial gain.'

'I see.'

'Do you, Matthew?' she pleaded hopefully, but Matthew's expression remained harsh. 'I suppose you realise that this is the mystery I still had to explain to you?'

'You may have made a fool of me, Tessa,' he exploded angrily, 'but I'm not a complete idiot!'

'I didn't intend making a fool of you,' she argued, her lips trembling, 'and I know you're not an idiot, but please don't be so angry.'

Matthew's cold glance swept down the length of her. 'What do you want me to do? Laugh about it?'

'No,' she shook her head and bit her lip to steady it. 'I would prefer your understanding to your anger.'

'My God, Tessa!' he exclaimed, pushing his fingers through his hair as he walked away from the desk, and from her. 'When I think of the things I said to you, and the way we treated you. You—Theresa Ashton-Smythe —have been a servant in our home, and treated as such most of the time! I know we paid you a salary which would make any ordinary girl feel like a queen, but you ...' His voice trailed into silence as his eyes raked her coldly. 'My God, you've made fools of us all!'

'Not all of you,' Tessa remarked dully. 'Your mother knew.'

This bit of information made him cease his restless pacing abruptly. 'She knew?' he asked incredulously. 'Then why the devil didn't she say so?'

'I only discovered this myself a few days ago.'

Matthew walked across to his desk and slumped into his chair. He lit a cigarette with hands that shook visibly, and sat staring angrily at the blotter before him. Tessa felt as though her legs would no longer carry her weight and she, too, subsided weakly into a chair.

'Matthew,' she began hesitantly. 'This makes no difference to us, does it?'

'I'll say it does!' he exclaimed furiously, drawing hard on his cigarette. 'It makes every difference!'

'It makes no difference to our love for each other,' she argued, stubbornly ignoring his remark. 'It doesn't alter anything!'

'It alters everything!' he insisted, a strange whiteness about his lips. 'How can I expect you to bury yourself on this farm for the rest of your life?'

'But this is what I want!'

'For how long?' he mocked cynically. 'A few months? A year perhaps?'

Tessa sighed heavily. 'Do you imagine that my love for you is such a paltry thing that it won't stand the test of time?' Her glance was pleading. 'Haven't I proved that I'm adaptable?'

Matthew did not appear to be listening as he struggled with his own thoughts. 'Everything is falling into place now. You *did* study music at university, that's

165

why you play so well. You've given several recitals in Johannesburg, if my memory serves me correctly.' He crushed his cigarette into the ashtray. 'I can't understand why I didn't recognise you. I can only think it was the short hair and ridiculous clothes that threw me off the track. I was suspicious of you from the very beginning, but you cleverly evaded my questions until I'd gone beyond the stage of wanting to discover the truth about you.' His eyes seemed to scorch her. 'Were you sent as a replacement for Miss What's-her-name?'

'No.'

The silence stretched agonisingly taut between them as they faced each other with Matthew's accusing glance slicing her to the core. 'How many lies am I still to uncover? Was there truth in anything you said?'

She understood instantly what he was referring to and the stab of pain to her heart made her wince. 'The lies I told were merely to hide my identity. When I said I loved you, I meant it.'

Matthew twisted the knife in her heart by laughing cynically. 'I'm beginning to wonder if you're capable of loving, and if you don't perhaps make a habit of pretending to care when you don't, in fact, know how.'

'You know that's not true!' she cried brokenly, tears blurring her vision.

'I wonder.'

Tessa controlled herself with difficulty. Tears would not help her now. 'Where did you find that press cutting?' she finally asked when her curiosity could no longer be contained.

'Angela gave it to me,' he replied bluntly. 'I'd asked her to do some delving for me, remember?'

166

Angela! She felt curiously hurt at the thought, but brushed it aside for the moment. Her happiness was at stake and she had to penetrate the hard crust Matthew had erected around him.

She rose to her feet and walked around the desk to kneel beside his chair. 'Matthew, I'm sorry. Please forgive me, but don't let it spoil things for us. Please, darling?'

He moved away from her then, thrusting her hands aside and leaving his chair to resume his restless pacing. 'There's no future for us together, and I suggest you leave first thing in the morning.'

'No!' A wave of panic engulfed her as she leaned against the desk for support. 'You can't be serious? You can't do this!'

'I can and I will!' he stated coldly. 'As far as you and I are concerned, we're finished.'

'Matthew, be sensible,' she begged, choking in the tears that could no longer be checked. 'You can't do this to me. I'll sue you for breach of promise,' she threatened as a last resort.

'You can't do that because I never asked you to marry me.'

His bluntness was brutal while he remained absolutely immovable on the subject. 'Oh, Matthew, I won't let you spoil or destroy our love.'

Tessa had the satisfaction of seeing his face go a shade paler, but the lips which could create such havoc with her emotions remained tight and unrelenting. 'Everything between us has already been destroyed by your deliberate deceit, and I think at this moment I could almost hate you!'

'No!'

It was like a physical blow that drove every vestige of colour from her face. She had known that he would be angry, but she would never have guessed that his pride would drive him this far. She searched his face for some sign that would indicate he had not meant what he had said, but there was none, except for that cold mask of indifference. She could take his anger, even his mockery, but indifference from Matthew was something she could not endure. With her world crashing about her, she had only one thing to cling to. Her pride! Pride had helped her through the embarrassment of being jilted, and it would have to help her now.

She drew a shuddering breath and faced him unflinchingly. 'I've never had to beg for anything in my life, and I don't intend to start now.' She swallowed at the constriction in her throat. 'If you really want me to go, then I will.'

Matthew turned his back on her and walked across to the window to stare out into the darkness, his hands thrust deep into his pockets. 'Believe me, it would be better that way. Better for both of us.'

She stared at his broad, forbidding back, and felt herself begin to shake uncontrollably. The tears rushed to her eyes and threatened to choke her. 'What—what will you tell your mother?'

'The truth,' he replied harshly. 'There'll be no more lies and deceit.'

Tessa stared at his unrelenting figure for a moment longer through a haze of tears before turning and stumbling blindly towards the door. He did not try to stop her and somehow she reached the privacy of her room before her rigid control snapped, and great heaving sobs racked her body as, without turning on the light, she threw herself across the bed and smothered the sound of her weeping in her pillow.

Her happiness had been all too brief. Barely a few hours ago, in this very room, they had shared a few precious moments together, moments during which she felt secure in the knowledge of his love. She had been so certain that, when she told him the truth, his love for her would overrule his anger; his understanding overruling his pride. As her tears dried on her lashes she laughed bitterly at her own naïveté. How sadly she had misjudged him, she thought, torturing herself further. She could appreciate his argument that she might eventually tire of the life he had to offer on a sugar plantation when she was so used to a social life, but surely if he had truly loved her this would not have been an insurmountable problem? Did he not know how little she cared for the life he was sending her back to?

The morning found Tessa packed and ready to leave. She had slept very little, but this did not trouble her, for she had decided to stop over somewhere along the way when tiredness overcame her. As she glanced briefly about the room to make sure that she had left nothing, there was a light tap at her door. She tensed instantly.

'Who is it?'

The door opened slightly. 'It's Barry. May I come in?'

Relieved, she walked across the room and opened the door to find a rather uncomfortable-looking Barry standing there.

'Come in, please. I'm just checking to make sure I haven't left anything behind.'

'So you're really leaving? It's not some sort of joke?'

Tessa glanced up into his troubled face, her expression guarded. 'Yes, I'm really leaving. I suppose you've heard why?'

Barry nodded, his expression darkening. 'What difference does it make? Underneath you're still the same person.'

Tessa drew a choking breath and stepped closed to him, placing her hands on either side of his face. 'You've been a very dear friend, and I shan't forget you.'

He removed her hands from his face and held them tightly. 'I think Matthew needs his head read, sending you away like this when any fool can see he's gone completely overboard for you.'

Her pulse drummed heavily against her temples. Did Matthew perhaps need time to adjust? If she could believe this, then she would leave with a lighter heart and give him all the time he needed if it meant their eventual happiness together.

'I was told to come and collect your suitcases,' Barry interrupted her thoughts. 'Matthew also told me to tell you that he's filled your car with petrol, so you should get quite far on a full tank.'

'Shan't I see him before I go?' Her blue eyes were wide and anxious.

Barry shrugged angrily. 'I saw him walking into the plantation a few minutes ago as though he felt like

170

tearing everything apart. When he's in that frame of mind, no one knows what he'll do, and no one questions him either.'

Tessa refrained from commenting and gave him the keys to her car. 'When you have put my suitcases in the boot, will you bring the car round to the front for me?'

He stared hard at her for a moment before taking the keys and marching out of her room with her suitcases, while Tessa followed more slowly.

'I refuse to let you go like this!' Mrs Craig announced angrily when Tessa went in to say goodbye. 'Matthew is allowing his stupid pride to overrule his better judgment.'

'Perhaps,' Tessa agreed quietly, 'but I'm going nevertheless.'

'But he loves you,' she persisted, her voice rising in desperation. 'I know he does!'

Tessa digested this calmly in the brief silence that followed. Then, persuading herself not to hope too much, she bent down and kissed Mrs Craig on the cheek. 'If Matthew really loves me, then I hope he won't be too proud to come to me.'

Mrs Craig caught at her hands. 'You won't send him away if he does, will you?'

Tessa shook her head. 'No, I shan't send him away.'

The garden was bathed in sunshine when Tessa stepped out on to the patio, but she was oblivious of the fact that so much beauty surrounded her. To her surprise, Matthew stood leaning against the bonnet of the Porsche as she approached and her heart lurched violently at the sight of him. Dear God, would she ever

171

be able to forget him? If he should discover that he did not love her enough, would she be able to live a lifetime without him?

'There's no need for you to go before you've had breakfast,' he said bluntly, avoiding her eyes.

'I would prefer to eat something along the way.'

He produced her cheque book from the back pocket of his slacks. 'You left this in my study last night.'

Their fingers touched lightly as she took it from him and her resolve to remain calm almost crumbled. 'Thank you.'

Their glances met for endless seconds of soul-searching that merely made the parting more painful, for both Matthew and Tessa had pulled down the shutters on the mirrors of their souls to hide what lay beyond, allowing stubbornness and pride to have a field day.

'Goodbye, Tessa.'

She started violently at the finality in his voice and suddenly she became daring. She slid behind the wheel of the Porsche and slammed the door before turning the key in the ignition and starting the engine. As Matthew stepped back from the car Tessa glanced up at him through the window, a tight smile on her lips at the bleakness in his expression. '*Tot siens*, Matthew. Till we meet again.'

The Porsche roared down the driveway and sped towards the main road through the cane fields. Tessa did not look back. She could not, lest her control should snap, and she was determined to show Matthew that she could be as proud and stubborn as he. But, despite

172

all her good intentions, her restraint crumbled several
kilometres from the farm and she had to pull off the
road to stem the flow of the terrible tears that ravaged
her face and left her weak and listless.

CHAPTER TEN

TESSA knew that there was only one thing which could help to take her mind off Matthew. At the first offer that she should give another recital, she accepted gladly and plunged into the preparations for this, not sparing herself for one moment. During the eight weeks she had been away, she had neglected her playing and as a result she was suffering the consequences, but this did not deter her, for it merely meant working harder at the piano, and while doing so she could forget that there ever was someone like Matthew Craig, if only for a few brief hours.

At first she could not speak of Matthew to her parents; the wound was too fresh to be discussed rationally and without shedding tears, and when at last she managed to speak of him, she found that she could not stop. He was in her thoughts every moment of every day, and so also did her dreams at night revolve around him. She discussed the situation with her parents until she was sure that they were sick to death of the subject.

'When are we going to meet this wonderful man of yours?' they kept asking.

'Soon, I hope,' she would reply. If he loved her, as she was almost sure he did, he would not stay away too long. Would he? Surely he would not allow his foolish pride to destroy his happiness, as well as hers?

Tessa had been home almost a month when she received a letter from Angela. At first she was reluctant to read it, but then her curiosity got the better of her and she slit open the envelope and extracted the letter with a slight feeling of anticipation.

'Dear Tessa,' Angela had written, 'Everyone has been rather reluctant to talk about you since your departure. Matthew stalks about looking like a threatening thunderstorm, and Barry bites my head off each time I show concern. When I ask for an explanation, Barry mumbles something about it being Matthew's own fault, and that I shouldn't waste my sympathy on him.

'I had quite a long discussion with Mrs Craig yesterday—she is missing you dreadfully, by the way—and it was only then that I realised how instrumental I actually was in your sudden departure. Tessa, I would like you to believe that I had no idea you were Theresa Ashton-Smythe when I gave that newspaper cutting to Matthew. As far as I was concerned, you merely resembled her. This sounds silly, but you know what I mean.

'Whatever it was that transpired between yourself and Matthew, he is not happy, and neither, I'm sure, are you. It's pride that made Matthew send you away, and it's pride that's preventing him from admitting his error. Mrs Craig, Barry and I have entered into a conspiracy. Whereas your name was never mentioned before, we shall now speak of you often, and hound Matthew with your memory. So take heart. Angela.'

Tessa felt tremendously lighthearted after reading that letter. She had not realised how much it had hurt her to think that Angela had deliberately intended to cause trouble between Matthew and herself. There was, of course, another reason for the warmth which had settled about her heart. Matthew was feeling just as miserable as she, if Angela's remarks could be taken seriously, and this knowledge alone gave her more hope for the future. Matthew would not be able to stay away for ever, she told herself with a new-found confidence.

Her step was light as she entered the music room and moments later she plunged into Rachmaninoff's Second Piano Concerto with more vigour than ever before. She practised tirelessly for three hours until the door opened and her mother entered with a tray of tea.

'You've done enough for this morning,' her mother said firmly, placing the tray on a small table and pouring their tea. 'If I hear another note before this afternoon, I shall scream!'

'I'm sorry, Mother.'

Sheila Ashton-Smythe glanced up at her daughter and smiled. 'You're playing well this morning. Has it perhaps anything to do with that letter you received from Idwala?'

'Yes, it has,' Tessa acknowledged, stirring her tea thoughtfully. 'It's not so much what was in the letter that's given me hope, but what I read between the lines.'

'Oh ... I see.'

'Do you, Mother?' Tessa laughed mischievously, and fished in the pocket of her slacks for Angela's letter. 'Read that, and tell me if I'm reading too much between the lines as well as allowing my hopes to soar too high.'

Sheila read through the letter carefully before returning it to Tessa. 'This Angela, is she the one you thought Matthew was in love with at first?'

Tessa nodded, emptying her cup. 'She's engaged to Barry now, and I presume they'll be married shortly.'

'Does Matthew love you?'

Tessa hesitated briefly. 'Yes.'

'Can you be sure of this?' her mother persisted.

'He said so.' Tessa bit her lip. 'Unless, of course, he goes about professing to love every girl he kisses, and Matthew isn't like that,' she ended confidently.

'Then you have nothing to worry about,' her mother smiled, pouring them each a second cup of tea.

She had nothing to worry about, yet as each day came and went she began to wonder if she did not indeed have something to worry about. She greeted each day with an air of expectancy that collapsed totally towards the afternoon when there was no sign of Matthew, and this situation continued until she found herself beginning to despair of ever seeing him again. She had been home almost as long as the length of her stay on the farm and surely, if he loved her, he could have taken the trouble to come and see her?

Perhaps they were busy on the farm. Perhaps he can't get away, she pacified herself. Oh, to the devil with Matthew! Why did she have to love him so?

Her first recital since her return home had been a success, the second even more so, but she refused to do a third, and no amount of persuasion could dissuade her from this decision. Her heart was no longer in what she was doing, and her incoherent thoughts filled her mind to the extent that there was room for

177

little else. The days were beginning to drag by, and on several occasions she very nearly succumbed to the temptation to telephone the farm and ask to speak to Matthew. If he could be stubborn, then so could she, she told herself firmly. *He* had sent her away, so *he* should make the first move.

Tessa was cleaning out the music room one afternoon and sorting through some old musical scores when the maid knocked at the door. 'There's a gentleman to see you, Miss Theresa.'

'Where is he?' Tessa asked, dropping a pile of music on to the piano and following the maid from the room.

'In the living-room, Miss Theresa.'

If this was another attempt to get her to agree to a third recital, she thought with tight-lipped determination, then she would tell whoever it was, in no uncertain terms, that she was not available.

The living-room door stood ajar and Tessa pushed it open further as she entered. The next instant she froze, her heart clamouring in her throat like a bird struggling for release. Standing at the french windows with his back to her was Matthew, his dark suit accentuating the fairness of his hair as it grew into his neck, and the unmistakable breadth of shoulders tapering down to slim hips.

'Matthew.' His name was a mere breath of a sigh on her lips, but it was loud enough for him to hear and he swung round to face her. Tessa could not recall afterwards what her thoughts had been at that moment. She was aware only of his dear, familiar face, and a flood of expectancy surging through her despite the fact that his expression held nothing promising for her.

178

'So, for the first time I see you as you really are.' His eyes swept over her, taking in every detail with a cynical twist to his lips. 'Theresa Ashton-Smythe unmistakably, from the stylishly cut hair down to the handmade, imported shoes. Added to which there's that expensive gold chain about your neck with the bracelet to match.' He came towards her then and fingered the sleeve of her dress. 'Genuine silk, I presume?'

Tessa's heart raced uncomfortably at his nearness. 'Have you come all this way merely to pass sarcastic remarks about my appearance?'

'No.' He dropped his hand to his side and stepped away from her with that familiar mockery in his eyes. 'I was merely marvelling at your ability to adapt yourself to your surroundings like a chameleon. At this moment you match the splendour of your surroundings to perfection, while on the farm you dressed in clothes that were inexpensive and unimposing. But then, of course, you were playing a part; indulging in deceit, as it were.'

Matthew, please!' At that moment she wanted to feel the strength of his arms about her more than anything in the world, but his attitude was forbidding and unapproachable.

Matthew bowed mockingly. 'My apologies for reminding you of something which you obviously found highly amusing at the time, but no doubt your amusement has waned slightly?'

She felt her unpredictable anger clamouring for an outlet. 'It wasn't my intention to amuse myself at the expense of others, and you know that.'

'Do I?' His eyebrows flew upwards in mock surprise. 'I'm finding it rather difficult to credit you with sincerity.'

Tessa winced inwardly, but succeeded in remaining outwardly calm. 'What's the reason for your visit?'

They stood facing each other with almost the entire length of the room between them, and although she could have bridged the gap between them with a few quick strides, that invisible barrier still remained firmly intact and impenetrable.

Matthew gestured angrily with his hands. 'I came because I wanted to see you, but now that I've seen you, I don't know why the hell I came.'

Tessa winced once more and bit back a sharp retort. It would not do to lose her temper at this critical stage. 'Would you like something to drink?' she asked.

'No, thank you.'

She gestured towards a delicately carved chair with its velvety gold upholstery. 'Then won't you please sit down?'

'The perfect hostess, aren't you?' he mocked. 'Charming and cool no matter what the circumstances.'

Tessa could no longer control the trembling of her legs, and she subsided weakly into a chair beside her while Matthew remained standing, towering above her with that arrogant tilt to his head. 'Matthew, I'm trying very hard to understand your attitude, and to keep my temper in check.'

'I'm surprised you haven't already pressed that discreetly hidden buzzer to have me thrown out,' he bit back relentlessly.

For one brief second his mask slipped and Tessa was surprised to discover that he was nervous. This discovery gave her a certain amount of courage.

'There are three reasons why I can't do that,' she told him calmly. 'Firstly, there's no hidden buzzer in this room; secondly, there's no one I could call to have you thrown out; and thirdly, you've done nothing yet that warrants such an action.'

He regarded her closely for a moment before fumbling in his pocket for his cigarette case and lighting one. 'I never thought I would get to see you as easily as this,' he remarked, drawing hard on his cigarette. 'I thought I would have to make an appointment.'

'Oh, Matthew!' There was gentle rebuke in her voice which did not escape him, for he cast her an angry glance.

'Where are your parents?' he asked.

'Father's at the office, and Mother's playing bridge at the home of a friend.' She resisted a silencing hand as his lips twisted sardonically. 'Now, don't pass any derisive remarks about the idle rich. My mother is not the bridge-playing sort, and this venture happens to be in aid of charity.'

'I never said a word,' he protested in mock innocence.

'But you can't deny that you were preening yourself for a cutting remark, can you?' She heaved an exasperated sigh and rose to her feet. 'Oh, Matthew, let's stop fencing with each other.'

Matthew's expression became guarded. 'I wasn't aware that I was fencing with you.'

Tessa gestured helplessly with her hands and then allowed them to fall limply into her lap. 'Let's go out into the garden.'

To her surprise Matthew offered no resistance to her

181

suggestion, but merely followed her in silence as she led the way through the french windows and out on to the terrace. They walked in subdued silence amongst the indigenous trees and shrubs while Matthew finished his cigarette and finally crushed it beneath the heel of his shoe.

'This is more like a park and not a garden,' he said, squinting into the September sun. 'I suppose it does end somewhere?'

'Yes,' she replied distractedly. 'There's a bench behind those trees that overlooks the fishpond. It's peaceful there, and secluded.' She was aware that Matthew glanced at her strangely and for some reason she felt ridiculously nervous. 'How is your mother?'

'Her leg has mended well.' He broke a leaf off the eucalyptus tree and crushed it between his fingers before sniffing at it lightly. 'She sends her regards.'

'I miss her.' Tessa bit her lip. 'And Barry?'

'Preparing for his wedding in a month's time,' he replied bluntly. 'I've bought his share in the farm and at the moment he's in the throes of buying his own property.'

So Barry has had his way at last, Tessa thought happily. The emperor of the estate has finally been convinced of his brother's stability. A smile tugged at her lips as she unwittingly used Barry's expression with regard to Matthew.

The bench she had mentioned stood beneath the overhanging branches of an old oak tree. She sat down at one end of the bench and Matthew joined her at the other end. The situation was not without humour, she thought suddenly.

'You didn't appear to be very surprised at my appearance this afternoon,' Matthew remarked, observing her closely.

Once again a smile threatened to tug at her lips. 'I ... knew you would come.'

'Oh?' His eyebrows rose sharply.

'There is a limit to everyone's endurance,' she explained bravely, 'and I was rapidly approaching mine.'

There was a glimmer of a smile in his eyes as he replied. 'So you assumed that when I reached mine, I would come running?'

Tessa lowered her dark lashes and veiled her eyes. 'Not exactly running, but I ... hoped you would come.'

Her heart was thudding heavily against her ribs as an uncomfortable silence settled between them. Down in the fishpond the goldfish swam about lazily and quite unperturbed by the tension in the atmosphere, while beyond the pond the finches continued their restless fluttering as they built their nests in the overhanging branches of the willow tree. It seemed incredible to Tessa that everything could continue so undisturbed while her own emotions were in a turmoil. Matthew's visit had been extremely unsatisfactory so far. She was not sure what she had expected, but she had certainly not imagined he would drive the wedge in further between them. She *had* hoped that he would come because he loved and needed her.

He got to his feet and walked down to the pond, and Tessa watched him closely as he lit another cigarette and stared moodily down into the water. What was he thinking? she wondered frantically, and then, almost as if he sensed her impatience, he turned and walked back towards her at a leisurely pace. He did not sit down again but remained standing a little distance from her, frowning and drawing hard on his cigarette.

'Tessa, you suggested a moment ago that we should stop fencing with each other, and I agree. Now that I've seen you again, in your own environment, I realise more fully the futility of my mission.'

Tessa's heart lurched. 'Matthew, I——'

'Please let me finish,' he interrupted sternly. 'I'm not a pauper, in fact, I could quite comfortably support a wife and family, but my wealth could never compare with that which you are accustomed to.'

'But I——'

'To me the sugar plantation is my life, and I can't alter that,' he continued as if she had not spoken and she could do nothing but stare at him miserably while he paced about restlessly. 'You come from an extremely wealthy family, and besides this you're exceptionally gifted and talented. It would be more than selfish of me to expect you to give all this up for the solitary life on the farm.' He flung his cigarette to the ground and crushed it beneath his heel before gesturing expressively with his hands. 'I'm trying to make you understand, Tessa, that my reasons for sending you away, and for taking so long in coming to see you, were not entirely based on pride. I can see the pitfalls of the future perhaps a little more clearly than you, and for your own sake, I want to avoid them. There can be no future together for us.'

The chattering of the birds in the willow tree seemed to reach a crescendo. 'Have I no say in this matter?' she asked quietly.

'I don't think so, Tessa,' he replied in a clipped, emotionless voice. 'One must be practical.'

'Aren't you at all curious to know what I expect from life?' Her voice shook slightly. 'Does my happiness not interest you at all?'

There was a touch of exasperation in his voice when he spoke. 'It's *your* happiness I'm thinking of!'

'Is it?' She raised her pale face to his. 'There is a certain irony in the situation. There have been only two men in my life—the first one wanted me for his own financial gain, and the second doesn't want me *because* of my wealth.' There was a touch of hysteria in her laughter. 'It's all ... rather funny, don't you think?'

'Stop that at once!' His voice was like a whiplash and she sobered instantly.

'Oh, Matthew, must there always be a price tag attached to happiness?' she sobbed out, unable to control herself much longer, she rose to her feet and stumbled blindly towards him, sliding her arms inside his jacket and pressing herself against him as she inhaled the familiar fragrance of shaving cream mingled with tobacco. She was behaving quite contrary to her nature, but she no longer cared. She slid her hands across his back and had the satisfaction of feeling him tremble against her.

'For God's sake, Tessa, don't do that!' he exclaimed, not touching her. 'I'm only human!'

'I'm glad to hear that,' she laughed tremulously, burying her face against his broad chest. 'I was beginning to think you weren't.'

His arms were about her then, warm and firm, and

nothing seemed to exist beyond the pressure of his lips as they took hers hungrily, causing her pulse rate to accelerate sharply. This was where she belonged, and this was where she intended to remain.

'Dear heaven, Tessa, if you know how much I want you!' he groaned softly as he held her away from him, his green eyes searching her face. 'Have you taken in anything I told you?'

'Yes, I have, and what's more I understand your point of view. But you're so wrong, my darling. All I want is to be with you.' She would have slipped into his arms once more, but he held her off firmly by the shoulders.

'What about your musical career?'

Tessa sighed and moved away from him then. 'To be quite honest, my parents would like me to be a concert pianist, but all I've ever wanted was to play for my own amusement, and to teach music.'

His glance was sceptical. 'You won't find much scope for that in Idwala.'

She gestured expressively with her hands. 'Whether I have one pupil or a hundred, it makes no difference.'

The atmosphere was heavily charged for a moment as they faced each other. 'If you should marry me, only to regret your decision afterwards, what then?' His eyes darkened and became somewhat threatening. 'I'd better warn you that, once you're married to me, I shall never let you go.'

Tessa drew a careful breath. 'Is this a proposal?'

'If you like.'

Every conceivable emotion seemed to clamour through her at that moment, but the most prominent was the feeling of intense relief and indescribable happiness.

'Oh, I do like!' she cried joyously, flying into his arms and burying her face against him. 'And the answer is ... yes, please.'

'Tessa, you must consider your decision carefully and sensibly,' he persisted, keeping a tight rein on his emotions.

'Matthew, I've been doing nothing else these past weeks,' she told him, her eyes bright and pleading. 'Aren't you ever going to tell me you love me?'

'Oh, my darling heart!' he exclaimed, scooping her up against him with a fierceness that was both an agony and a joy. 'I love you so much that I've been absolutely terrified at the thought that you might tell me you've stopped caring.'

'I could never stop loving you, Matthew,' she sighed ecstatically after he had kissed her with lingering passion. 'Not even your boorishness could alter that, and you were positively boorish when you arrived.'

'I know,' he acknowledged readily, quite unperturbed by the glimmer of amusement in her eyes. 'I was uncertain, and everything looked so imposing and intimidating. You walked in then, and you looked so lovely, and so much a part of it all, that I was certain I'd already lost.'

'So you lashed out in self-defence before you were even attacked.'

'Something like that.' His lips moved across her cheek towards her ear. 'Will you marry me, Tessa?'

'You know the answer to that question,' she whispered.

His lips explored further along the column of her throat towards her shoulder, sending delicious little tremors rushing through her. 'When?'

'As soon as you like.'

'I presume it will have to be a big wedding?' he said some time later as he sat on the bench with his arms about her.

Tessa laughed happily, pressing her head on to his shoulder. 'After the fiasco we went through once before, I'm certain my parents will agree to a quiet wedding somewhere inconspicuous, and with as little publicity as possible.'

Matthew stiffened instantly. 'Oh, lord, I never thought of the publicity!'

'If we behave very discreetly, we could quite possibly avoid it,' she assured him gently.

Matthew's expression remained tense. 'Do you think your parents will consent to our marriage?'

'I'm over twenty-one.'

'I'll ask them nevertheless,' he declared firmly.

'Matthew, my darling, it will come as no surprise to them,' she whispered, trailing a lazy finger along the firm line of his jaw and rejoicing in the thought that her touch would no longer be rejected. 'They know all about you, and they've been so anxious to meet you.'

He caught her hand and pressed his lips to the delicate network of veins at her wrist while his eyes appraised her teasingly. 'I presume they would like to give me the once-over?'

'No, darling,' she laughed up at him. 'To beg you, if necessary, to take this miserable daughter of theirs off their hands.'

He lowered his head and took the lips she was offering. 'Do you think they might object if I suggest marrying you before the end of this week?'

'No.'

Matthew stood up then and pulled her to her feet. 'Have *you* any objections?'

'Oh, no. No, I haven't,' she whispered dreamily as she moved back into the circle of his arms. There was now a sudden urgency in the pressure of his lips and the touch of his hands as they caressed her wildly. Flushed and trembling, she was eventually forced to hold him at bay with her hands against his chest. 'I—I think we'd better go indoors once more. If the gardener should see us now, he would think us positively indecent!'

'And with reason,' he laughed, trailing a finger along her warm cheek. 'Tessa, are you sure——'

Swiftly she placed her fingers against his lips and shook her head in gentle reprimand. 'I've never been more sure of anything in my life. She reached up and kissed him lightly on the lips. 'No more doubts, my darling. Please?'

The sun was losing its warmth and casting long shadows across the lawns as they strolled back towards the house with their arms about each other. Neither of them noticed the slight drop in the temperature, for no one ever does when they are basking in the warmth of their love. They were also totally oblivious of the two people watching their approach from the living-room window. On the table in the centre of the room, a bottle of champagne nestled amongst the ice-cubes, and beside it a box of the best cigars stood open and waiting.

Mills & Boon Reader Film Service

See your pictures before you pay

Our confidence in the quality of our colour prints is
such that we send the developed film to you
without asking for payment in advance. We bill
you for only the prints that you receive, which
means that if your prints don't come out, you won't
just be sent an annoying credit note as with the
'cash with order' film services.

Free Kodacolor Film

We replace each film sent for processing with a
fresh Kodacolor film to fit the customer's camera
without further charge. Kodak's suggested prices in
the shops are:

110/24 exp. £1.79
126/24 exp. £1.88
135/24 exp. £1.88
135/36 exp. £2.39

Top Quality Colour Prints

We have arranged for your films to be developed by
the largest and longest established firm of mail
order film processors in Britain. We are confident
that you will be delighted with the quality they
produce. Our commitment, and their technical
expertise ensures that we stay ahead.

How long does it take?

Your film will be in their laboratory for a maximum
of 48 hours. We won't deny that problems can
occasionally arise or that the odd film requires

Mills & Boon Reader Film Service

special attention resulting in a short delay.
Obviously the postal time must be added and we
cannot eliminate the possibility of an occasional
delay here but your film should take no longer than
7 days door-to-door.

What you get

Superprints giving 30% more picture area than the
old style standard enprint. Print sizes as follows:

Print Size	from 35mm	from 110	from 126
Superprints	$4'' \times 5\frac{3}{4}''$	$4'' \times 5\frac{1}{8}''$	$4'' \times 4''$

All sizes approximate.
All prints are borderless, have round corners and a
sheen surface.

Prices

No developing charge, you only pay for each
successful print:
Superprints   22p each.
This includes VAT at the current rate and applies to
100 ASA film only. Prices apply to UK only. There is
no minimum charge.
We handle colour negative film for prints only and
Superprints can only be made from 35mm, 126 and
110 film which is for C41 process.

If you have any queries 'phone 0734 597332 or
write to: Customer Service, Mills & Boon Reader
Film Service, P.O. Box 180, Reading RG1 3PF.